My Everything

Blackhawk Chronicles

Book Two

by
Alane Hotchkin

Affinity
eBook Press
NZ
2014

My Everything
© 2014 by Alane Hotchkin

Affinity E-Book Press NZ LTD.
Canterbury, New Zealand

1st Edition

ISBN: 978-1-927282-44-1

All rights reserved

No part of this e-Book may be reproduced in any form without the express permission of the author and publisher. Please note that piracy of copyrighted materials violate the author's rights and is Illegal.

This is a work of fiction. Names, character, places, and incidents are the product of the author's imagination or are used fictitiously and any resemblance to actual persons living or dead, businesses, companies, events, or locales is entirely coincidental

Editor: Nat Burns
Cover Design: Irish Dragon Designs

Acknowledgments

It has been a long road to get here. There are so many people that deserve to be applauded. First and foremost the entire crew at Affinity. They have given me a chance to put my words into print to share with the rest of the world and I will be forever grateful for that.

I want to thank my betas, especially Joe and TJ. The late e-mails and long conversations are appreciated beyond words. They are the best in the world.

Lori as always – thank you and I bow to you.

The cover is a work of art due to Nancy. It amazes me how she can capture the essence of the story in a picture.

And of course to my Sarah…thank you for loving me.

Dedication

Love can conquer almost anything. There are the rare times though when an individual must come to terms with the raw reality of life. This is for all those women and men who stand up and say—"Enough, I deserve better. "

And to my wife, Sarah my heart belongs to you.

Table of Contents

Introduction   1

Prologue   2

Chapter One   4

Chapter Two   53

Chapter Three   91

Chapter Four   127

Chapter Five   168

Chapter Six   215

Epilogue   245

About the Author   247

Other Books from Affinity   248

Introduction

By
Lillith Blackhawk

Welcome back to the Blackhawk Chronicles.

Nikki gave me so much, she gave me life again. I learned through her love that sometimes family is not what you were born into but those you gather along your travels. When I lost my own blood family so long ago, I became a tool for others to wield.

For every good in the world there is evil, one must just find the balance. She balances me, even when I stray off course. Nikki is my path and my way home.

In the end we all stand alone in judgment of our souls. You must find the one true soul that makes you worthy.

This is how all the pieces began to fall into place. First was the call for help, then I fell into those eyes and I knew…

I reached into the blackness of the deeds I had done only to find that I did indeed have a heart and soul once again.

LB

Prologue

Many years ago, in a dark place in a second floor closet, an eight year old girl sat on the hard floor crying. Dinner had long since been finished. The enticing smells of her mother's cooking had long since faded away.

Having missed her evening meal, the little girl's tummy rumbled and hurt. It was not the first to be missed, nor would it be the last. The same held true for the punishment time spent locked in the dark closet.

"Please daddy, please may I come out? I have to go potty." The urgent little voice called into the dark.

The little girl's words went unanswered. Knowing what would happen if she had an accident, the frightened reddish-brown haired child held it as long as she could. Tears streamed down her face as pure fear took her.

Not able to hold it any longer, she wet her new Easter dress and panties.

As Nikki grew so did her abject fear of the dark and of life itself. The punishments grew more severe as the step-father did what he thought any child deserved. He would beat the wicked ways from her body until she submitted and repented her sins.

As an adult Nikki longed for love and acceptance. She would do anything, accept any scraps of attention thrown her way, never questioning the outcome. Nikki lived in a fog until a hand reached through and pulled her home.

Chapter One

Relax and Breathe

It still seemed so unreal to them that they had lived in their new home for more than two years. It felt as if it was yesterday that Alex's parents had passed away. Slowly the house felt as if it belonged to them. Yet, it wouldn't matter if they lived there for the next eighty years, Alex would always think of it as Alice and Tony's house.

Alex had cussed her parents out many times during the past few months, since inheriting the house. She couldn't understand why her father hadn't taken care of the little things or why he didn't call her to help with the bigger items, like painting the exterior. She would've been there in a heartbeat, if only he'd asked.

Their death had happened so suddenly, so abruptly, and had bewildered all. Tony and Alice were on their way to meet friends for breakfast when destiny intervened. Destiny and a truck driver who fell asleep at the wheel.

The accident that morning took more than those three lives. It took the last remaining shred of humanity from one tortured soul. As others sat weeping openly at the funeral service and again at the gravesite, Alex sat frowning, vowing to find their killer in hell and torture him throughout all eternity, to make him suffer the same as she was suffering.

Alex dealt with the sudden loss by not letting the sorrow in. Nikki thought of her lover as strong. She never knew the truth. It was self-hatred Alex had truly been feeling and still did. Alex felt it was her fault her parents had been claimed in the accident. That it was the Fates passing judgment on her for cheating on Nikki.

†

Prior to moving in, Alex had the hardwood floors refinished and painted several of the rooms. The first room they drastically changed in appearance was the kitchen. It was in dire need of a makeover. The room still had the fifties motif from when Alex's parents bought it from her father's parents.

Nikki wanted a large kitchen, so they made expanding the current one their main priority. Scott helped Alex remodel the kitchen. However, he recommended someone else do the new cabinets. Taking her design to the cabinetmaker, Alex was impressed when he immediately grasped her concept. It was during that time that she decided to go to her favorite store in Charlotte and purchase all new appliances. She made sure they were top of the line stainless steel.

Alex built a large island with a special built-in knife rack which Nikki thanked her for many nights afterwards. Nikki loved her island and loved Alex more every day. Completion of the kitchen took a week longer when the new counter tops, made of top-of-the-line granite, were late being delivered. Alex spared no expense in the remodeling of Nikki's studio, as she called it.

After living in their new home for a month, Alex designed a new deck for the back. Luckily for them, the end of April was unseasonably warm. Their good fortune continued when the concrete company was able to pour the footers right away and Alex was able to start construction immediately. When halfway done, she had to have them come back and pour four more footers. Somehow, when she was finished building it a month later, it was twice the size as the plans for it. She had even built into it a special alcove for her massive stainless steel, special-order gas grill.

To Nikki it looked more like an industrial size-cooking stove complete with every gadget known to man. She didn't care though. It had brought such joy to Alex the morning that the truck had backed up into their driveway to make the delivery. She was like a kid with a new set of Legos® and of course, they had to grill on it that very night. Alex refused to wait, pouting like a two year old until Nikki agreed.

While designing the deck, Alex had also worked on redesigning the windows on the back of the house that looked out onto the deck and backyard. That project of course expanded into new windows for the whole house the day Alex heard a loud crash and swearing coming from one of the upstairs bedrooms. Nikki had been trying to close one of the open windows in the spare bedroom when it came crashing down, causing the glass to shatter.

The windows were not only ugly, they were misaligned and let in cold air. On top of all that, they proved to be dangerous because in the entire house, only one window locked. Due to the misalignment, the locks were useless.

While replacing the deck, Alex came up with an idea for the back room. It took her another two weeks to find the perfect contractor. Alex wanted someone who could not only do the windows, but the structural work needed for a large bay window.

Finally, four months after moving in, the house looked and felt like a home to them. The contractor was a day at most from being finished.

Alex walked from room to room inspecting the work, ending with the room in the back. She found Nikki admiring the large bay window with a bench seat for watching wildlife in the backyard.

Both had taken vacation time off and on, to be there during the process. Nikki wanted to be there because she found the transformation fascinating. Alex was there to keep an eye on the work being done and a watchful eye over Nikki. She didn't trust people she didn't know alone with her girlfriend.

✝

Starting with the kitchen being renovated, then the deck, it snowballed out of control. The bedroom – bathroom would be the last project, Nikki hoped, for quite some time. Alex picked out everything from the tile color, right down to the soap dish for the wall in the shower.

Before beginning, Alex hired an inspector to make sure everything was secure enough for the new tub. She opened up the bedroom wall between theirs and the one next to it to make one extra-large room. Since it was not a load-bearing wall, they could do the work themselves.

Nikki was ecstatic when Scott helped Alex install the Jacuzzi tub in the corner by the new walk-in closet. She was tired of looking at it sitting in the spare room. When they had the windows redone, Alex had gone ahead and had the tub delivered. It made it much easier bringing it in through the second floor windows than trying to go up the stairs.

Alex loved doing all the work and Scott took instruction well. She would've done the remodel of the back room also, but they were changing the exterior structure. Alex didn't want to chance it herself.

Alex found herself being more attentive to Nikki's needs and desires. Alex made sure she wanted for nothing. When Nikki mentioned she saw something she liked, Alex would run out and buy it for her. Sometimes she would give it to her the next day, others she'd wait a week or two. Alex only hoped Nikki would never question her on it.

Nikki in turn became more attentive toward Alex. Deep in her sub-conscious, she had an inkling that Alex hadn't told her everything from that night. Nikki felt that if she gave into all of Alex's whims, she would never have a need to look elsewhere. Since that night, Alex had lost her temper a handful of times, twice leaving several bruises on her arms and then on her neck when the make-up sex became a little rough.

†

All had been going well when Nikki's life was thrown into a spin. She had not expected it when it happened, it was just so sudden. It was true, there was no love lost between Nikki and her sister, but she had never wished Millie's death. It had been such a shock that Nikki became depressed. Of course, the depression only lasted a couple of days. Yes, she was upset, but why should she waste her life on someone who couldn't have cared less if she herself was alive and breathing?

When she received the call from the doctor asking her to come to the hospital, she was puzzled, asking what it was about. It couldn't have been Alex. She was in the living room watching a hockey game. When he told her that her sister had passed away, her response startled him, however, he chalked it up to shock.

Nikki said the first thing that popped into her mind. "Good, I won't have to tolerate her hatred any longer."

It saddened Nikki to lose her last remaining relative. What grated on her more though, was she never had the chance to tell Millie how much she truly loathed her. She chastised herself for feeling that way. Nikki told herself that Millie was her sister, so she should love her no matter what. She just couldn't do it though. During the several days that followed, Nikki's emotions were a roller coaster, which in turn drove Alex mad.

†

Alex tried to understand what Nikki was going through. She, however, couldn't quite get to that point. Alex hated Millie and what she had done to Nikki. She'd wished Millie dead many times and now that she was, she couldn't understand why Nikki was upset.

Saturday night, two weeks after the funeral, Nikki was supposed to be ready at seven. They were going out to dinner with Scott and Tessa. It was already seven-thirty and she still wasn't ready. Alex was furious. She hated being late and felt it made her personally look bad.

Finally, she'd had enough, yelling at Nikki to, as she put it, 'get her fucking ass in gear', or they were going to be even later.

Sitting on the end of the bed, Nikki listened to Alex pace while ranting and raving at the bottom of the steps. "Alex, I'm hurrying, I just don't really feel like going out. I have quite a bit of work to do still tonight and I've got a raging migraine."

Nikki knew Alex had already been drinking. She was in no mood to deal with a drunken lover this evening. She still had too much work to do before the night was done.

"We already agreed to go to dinner with them, so just get your ass moving. You making us late is going to embarrass me once again, and I won't tolerate that."

Alex polished off the beer she was working on and got another one out, as she heard Nikki walking down the steps to the kitchen.

"I'm sorry Alex. I don't mean to make us late. I wanted to wear my red blouse but I think my red bra is down stairs in the dryer, I'll just go down and get it, and then I'll be ready to go." Walking through the living room, Alex grabbed her arm when she passed her.

"Finish getting dressed and I'll get it for you." She pushed Nikki aside.

Following Alex into the kitchen, Nikki touched her arm. "Alex it's okay, I can get it."

Without a moment's notice, Alex turned on her. "I said I'd *fucking get it!*"

Nikki didn't think about what happened next. She took a step toward Alex to try to calm her down. "Alex…" The next thing Nikki knew she was flying down the basement steps.

Nikki suffered minor bruises and a broken wrist.

✝

It had been six weeks since the accident. Nikki was supposed to get the cast off first thing Monday morning and Alex couldn't wait. The evidence of her injury only added more guilt onto Alex's already broken spirit.

Every morning when she woke, seeing the cast, was a reminder of what she'd done. Alex still couldn't remember what happened. One minute Nikki was walking by her, the next she was flying down the stairs. Alex was thankful that it was only a broken wrist, but to her it couldn't get any worse. She knew she was out of control and needed to do something about it. She just hoped that Nikki wouldn't leave her because of it.

After that night, Alex watched her drinking. She thought if she cut back, she wouldn't lose her temper as easily. Alex tried harder to offer Nikki the support she deserved. It was after that incident that she started the bathroom project. Alex was doing the bathroom for herself as much as for Nikki. It was her therapy of a sort. If she kept herself busy, she was less likely to get herself into trouble.

†

The new bathroom was almost finished. The last step was installing the marble tile surrounding the tub and Alex planned to have it done by dinnertime. Nikki's sister-in-law Kirstin and her entourage were set to arrive within two hours and she was getting close to being finished. She had surprised Nikki by taking vacation time in order to get the room done.

Nikki was under a great deal of stress at work so Alex tried very hard not to add to it. Nikki knew she was on her best behavior. The advertising agency

Nikki worked for was expanding every day and there were only so many hours in a day to get work done.

At the quarterly partners' meeting, Nikki requested another body for her department. She discussed it with Mark and he gave her his full support. It surprised her that the owners didn't even second-guess her. They just approved it outright. Before the higher ups could change their minds, she called the newspaper with an ad for the weekend edition.

Nikki was stressing about who to hire as her assistant. She couldn't have cared less what the person, male or female, looked like. She just wanted them to be able to do their job. She also wanted someone who was tolerant of, not only her lifestyle, but the other little things in the office area.

When deadlines were crashing down, it could get more than a little hectic. The office could get downright violent at times. A few times tempers flared and things were flung around the office. No one took it personally and they always laughed about it an hour or so later. They would then all go for drinks, the first round being on the person who had lost their temper first. The agency was a family that just got a little rowdy occasionally was how Nikki looked at it.

During dinner, Nikki had told Alex the good news.

"That is great, Nikki. Now you'll have a full time assistant. I like your idea of hiring someone who has little or no previous experience in the field. That way they have no bad habits that would need breaking. You can train her the way you see fit," Alex said.

"Mark asked if I would consider interviewing his niece for the job. She was laid off from the company she had been with for five years. I felt funny about saying no, so I didn't. I'll give her the same shot as the others. I just don't want to be accused of playing favoritism."

"Baby, everything will work out. Call her in for an interview. It's not like you'd be giving her the job without one."

Nikki hoped his niece wouldn't want the position anyway. Nikki wasn't too keen on family members working together. After a long internal debate, she called her only to receive an answering machine.

Nikki left her cell number for the woman to call her back. The voice on the answering machine piqued her curiosity to see what the woman was like. Her friend, Liz, had teased her, telling her that knowing her luck, she would be a mousy, shy little creature, with horn-rimmed glasses and buck teeth. Unfortunately, she received that precise image from the voice on the answering machine.

Nikki went back to filling the dishwasher with their dinner dishes. The doorbell rang causing her to jump. "I'll get it," Nikki yelled.

Opening the door she found no one there, only an envelope laying on their doormat. Closing the door, Nikki tore open the envelope.

Hearing her name screamed, Alex ran to see what was wrong. She found Nikki leaning against the front door with a sheet of paper in her hand, the envelope lying on the floor. "Babe, what's wrong?"

Tears in her eyes, she looked up at Alex. "It's awful, the things in this letter."

Alex took the paper from Nikki's hand. Reading it, she became angry. It laid out all Alex's past liaisons with women. "I'll take this to Mahoney. There's something not right about it."

She kissed Nikki on the lips, picked up the envelope and left for the station.

✝

The next afternoon Nikki stood in the doorway watching Alex installing the new shower head. She admired her lover's body. The way her muscles moved.

Alex had on an old pair of ratty black shorts, which had seen better days, and a black muscle tee shirt. Her hair was pulled back into a ponytail to keep it out of her face as she worked. Nikki could have stood there watching her for longer and would have if Alex had not noticed her presence.

Alex looked up and smiled. She could feel Nikki watching her. It was one of the things that made her such a good cop—instinct. You were either born with it or not. If you didn't have it, more than likely you would die on the streets in no time. Alex believed it kept her alive and out of trouble in many ways.

That same instinct helped Alex sort of make friends with Nikki's best friend, Liz. She still didn't like her but knew that she and Nikki were close. Scott had reinforced, on several occasions that it was in her best interest to get along with Liz.

Alex looked up at her once again, after setting the tile she had cut.

Nikki saw the wetness in her eyes. "You okay? It looks like you're almost finished with the tile. It's beautiful." She put her hand on Alex's shoulder.

Alex leaned into Nikki, resting her head on her lover's thigh. "I'm almost finally done with this part, about twenty more minutes. Then all that's left to do is grout. I'll grab a shower in the other bathroom then I'll be down." She looked up at her questioningly, "I have enough time right?"

Running her fingers through Alex's bangs, she pulled them off her forehead. "You have plenty of time love. The only thing left to do is put the steaks on the grill once everyone gets here. The salads and corn are ready to go, so just relax and don't worry about a thing. It's all taken care of. I'll get the plates and stuff ready while you're finishing up here." Nikki kissed her on the forehead before leaving.

"I'll be along shortly babe. I'll start the grill when I come down."

Nikki smiled. "If you want me to start it for you, just yell down and I'll take care of it."

✝

Alex's sister, Kirstin, stayed in the kitchen to help Nikki with the rest of the food. Tom helped Alex with the grilling. The kids were in the pool. Nikki watched the kids out the kitchen window, thinking for a moment how nice it would be to have their own children. She pushed the feelings back down to where it came from. Alex made her thoughts on that subject very clear. She didn't want children. End of story.

She felt someone behind her.

"Have you tried to talk to her again about having children?" Kirstin stood by her and watched as the little terrors splash one another.

"I tried a couple of times, but it was the same answer. No, end of discussion. So that seals that matter closed. It's okay though, I can always borrow yours when I want to go to a kid's movie."

Nikki tried to act as if it didn't bother her, but Kirstin knew better. She knew she hurt. She noticed that the cast wasn't off yet.

"And…you're okay with that?"

"I have to be, don't I? I really don't have a choice." Nikki looked down at the floor.

Kirstin shook her head, sighing. There was always a choice. She would try a different approach to get Nikki to open up to her. "How's the wrist?"

Nikki held the cast up to look at it as if she was inspecting it. "It's healing. The doctor said even after I get the cast off, it will be a while before I get full strength back in it."

Kirstin laid her hand on Nikki's shoulder. "Nikki, are you sure that everything is okay? Has anyone ever mentioned anything to Alex about posttraumatic stress disorder? I've been reading up on it and I think maybe it explains a lot."

Nikki knew what she was hinting at. Kirstin was the first one to accuse Alex of being the cause of her getting hurt, then all the others followed suit.

"Kirstin, everything's fine. Why won't you believe me when I tell you that it was not Alex's fault? As for PTSD, I've never seen any of those symptoms in Alex. Please let's just relax and have a nice dinner. Please? For me?" Picking up the bowl of salad, Nikki headed for the door.

Her sister-in-law meant well. Kirstin was always the voice of reason. She was the glue that held the family together. This time however, Nikki's last nerve on the subject was frayed and Kirstin was twanging it like a rubber band.

"I'm sorry Nikki but I'm just a little gun shy believing what you told us, knowing what Alex is capable of." Kirstin followed behind her after grabbing another round of beers for everyone.

"No, Kirstin, I'm the one who is sorry. Sorry that it happened in such a boring way as me carrying a laundry basket downstairs and not watching where I was going, instead of what you're thinking. I know you would love for it to be a juicier story so you could blame it on her, but it wasn't her fault. Alex loves me like no other ever could. I'll never find anyone better than Alex. Can we drop it now, please?"

Their eyes met. In that split second, Kirstin knew she was lying and Nikki knew that she knew. However, nothing could be done. If anything was said, it would only send Alex off into a rage. "Okay change of subject then, are you doing any interviews tomorrow and any good prospects in them?"

Nikki was thankful for Kirstin finally taking the hint. She loved the woman dearly, but a person could only take so much.

"I have three each day for the next three days, including Mark's niece. It's really too soon to tell if any of them will work out. I'm looking for a, how do I put it, fresh face. I want someone who comes without baggage. One tomorrow I think already has some and if that is the case, no thanks." Nikki smiled at Alex, knowing that she was watching them talk.

She could feel the eyes on her, always watching, always seeing.

Dinner was the usual crazy affair it was when having children and Alex at the same table. Alex was nothing more than a large kid herself at times.

Turning in early, both fell asleep as soon as their heads hit the pillow. Nikki was thankful for the kids wearing Alex out, that way she could not grill her on what she and Kirstin had been talking about.

†

The week started off badly when the doctor thought the cast needed to stay on another two weeks. The x-rays taken through the cast showed the break not to have quite healed enough to satisfy the doctor. Nikki knew what the doctor's prediction would be without hearing it, especially how her morning had started.

Before leaving for her doctor's appointment, she went to the kitchen to retrieve her cell phone and keys. Neither were where she had left them.

"I'm positive I put the phone on its charger last night and my key ring on its hook by the door. I do it every single night when I get home. It's become a ritual so much that I even reach for the hook when Alex drives. Where the heck are they?" Nikki thought aloud. She searched everywhere, coming up empty handed.

"Duh, why don't I just call the phone?" Nikki heard ringing on the back deck. "Good Lord, I must have been tired last night. I must have taken them out onto the deck when I went to find Alex."

When it happened again two days later, she questioned Alex if she had moved them.

Alex's anger flared. "How dare you accuse me of doing something so childish! Maybe if you weren't so scatter-brained you'd remember where you left things."

A better idea occurred to Alex. This was working out perfectly, she wanted Nikki as a stay at home girlfriend and this was a prime opportunity to make a point. "Maybe you're working too hard. I think you need to quit this job. Your only job should be to take care of your girlfriend, which would be me."

"Alex once my projects are done and I get someone hired, why don't we take a vacation? Someplace to relax and do nothing for a week, what do you say?"

"I still think you don't need this job. It's too much stress on you. I'll agree to it only if you take two weeks off though."

Nikki smiled. She'd luckily diffused Alex's anger without much of a confrontation. "Okay two weeks then."

†

To further Nikki's miserable week, her first interview was a disaster. She caught him lying within the first ten minutes of the interview. He tried telling her he went to the same college that, unbeknownst to him, she had attended. To make matters worse for him, he told her he graduated the same year as she. Knowing everyone she graduated with, Nikki knew he was lying. It was not very encouraging considering he was the one of the three that had sounded the best.

Then several of the interviewees were no shows. Wednesday afternoon arrived and the last one was waiting to be shown in.

"Damn this is so frustrating. None of them are looking promising." Shaking her head in frustration, she continued talking to herself, which she seemed to do a lot of lately.

Nikki studied the resume once more before having the receptionist show her in. "Rory Scarpella. It's an interesting name at least. God, I really hope she's not a loser like the others. Somehow, I don't think she will be, seeing as she is Mark's niece. I'm just not sure I'd feel comfortable hiring her. Damn!"

She buzzed the receptionist. "Please show Ms. Scarpella in."

The office door opened and she looked up. Nikki was not prepared, for the door opening so fast. She was momentarily stunned at the first sight of Rory. Nikki covered the shock quickly. She didn't want the woman to think she was rude for just sitting there and staring at her, or worse, think she was giving her the once over.

The woman that stood before her resembled her knight in shining armor. One that had rescued her in many of her nightmares and carried her away from the fires of hell on her metal horse. Only Rory was of a slighter build.

The woman before her stood more than six feet tall. She had midnight black hair, pulled away from her face in a French braid, and the most amazing blue eyes. The woman had an aura about her that said 'Don't screw with me, because I can snap you like a twig'. Nikki was sure that under the suit jacket, there was strength to back up that attitude.

Nikki extended her hand as she stood. "Hello, I'm Nikki McLoud, please come in and have a seat."

The woman walked across the room as if she owned it. Rory looked at the cast and frowned. Nikki knew exactly what she was looking at and cast her eyes downward. The other woman took her hand. It was a warm, almost hot, yet gentle handshake.

"Rory Scarpella. It's nice to meet you." Rory looked at Nikki's arm then their eyes met. She knew by the barren look in Nikki's eyes that she had more than likely been hurt on purpose.

"Why don't we start out with what you think you can bring to the company."

Their eyes met.

"I bring loyalty."

Nikki heavily sat in her chair. One thought screamed through her mind…*She knows.*

An hour later Nikki opened her office door to show Rory to the lobby. She shook her hand once more. Rory's hand lingered. Nikki looked up to see blue eyes almost turned violet, looking down at her.

Nikki cleared her throat before trying to speak. "I, um, I'll call you by Friday to let you know what I decide."

†

Three hours later Nikki still sat at her desk. She was worried. "Shit, out of all the people I interviewed, Rory's the only one with any potential. I really don't think I should hire her though."

Nikki didn't want to be accused of playing favoritism due to Rory was the bosses niece and she knew how Alex would react to such a good-looking woman working for her.

The second thought plagued her more than the first. She hadn't been able to concentrate on work after meeting Rory and as a result had accomplished nothing the rest of the day. Nikki noted that she had caught her looking at the cast twice during the interview, yet she said nothing. Rory didn't even ask what had happened.

Rory's single word kept replaying in her mind all afternoon.

Loyalty. *It was as if she was looking right through me. My gut instinct says yes, my brain says don't be that stupid. God, what am I going to do?"*

Unable to make a decision right then, she would have to think about it for a day or two. Packing up her files and laptop, she headed home to start dinner for Alex.

✝

Arriving home, she found Alex already at work in the bathroom, completing the final step which was grouting the tiles on the floor.

Alex grumbled as she worked. "Shit, this stuff is gross! Give me a fucking bloody crime scene any day. At least that I don't have to touch. Eww…"

Nikki leaned against the door much as she had less than a week ago, watching her. She hadn't seen Alex since the morning before. Alex called to say they were working a bad case that had just come in and that she would probably be there all night.

Nikki stood admiring her lover, trying to push down the desire that welled up every time she saw Alex's muscled body. Her eyes traveled down Alex's body slowly, admiring every square inch of her. The black muscle T-shirt, the boxer shorts…all made her heart race a little faster. Nikki's eyes landed on Alex's right arm and hand.

✝

Alex concentrated on grouting, letting her mind drift. She never knew anyone was behind her until she heard the gasp. Alex swiveled around in a defensive crouch with the trowel in her hand, ready to strike.

"Fuck, Nik, you scared the shit out of me. What the hell were you thinking sneaking up behind me like that?" Alex realized she was screaming at Nikki and felt instantly ashamed. She sat back on the floor, letting the anger seep from her body. "I'm sorry babe, you just scared me."

"Alex, uh… your arm. When did you…why did…a dragon?" Nikki couldn't form a complete sentence. She just stared at Alex's inked arm.

"Do you like it? We had a scene on Main, across from the tattoo place, so Scott and I hopped in while we were there." She held her arm up for Nikki to see. Right below her elbow, on the inside of her lower arm, started the dragon's head and body. Its tail wound its way around her arm and hand.

"It's beautiful, I admit, but why?" She seemed not to comprehend why Alex would get a tattoo of a dragon on her arm.

"Why not? I've always loved dragons. I think it's awesome." She saw the puzzled look still on Nikki's face. "Why did you get the ones on your ass or on your shoulder? Cause you wanted them right? Well, I've always wanted one of a dragon. It kind of goes with the sword down the middle of my back, you know."

†

Nikki saw the smile on Alex's face. She knew she was being teased about one in particular on her rear, of a smiley face. She had always found the little yellow smiley face funny, so she had it tattooed on the opposite side from the yin/yang symbol. Nikki couldn't stifle the chuckle.

Alex looked up at her with a questioning look.

"Sorry, I am thinking of Smiley. Yes, I can understand it I guess, but why on your arm?" Nikki sat on the floor next to Alex. Drawing her finger down the edge of the tattoo, she was careful not to touch it, knowing it was still fresh and sore.

She contemplated for a moment before answering, trying to reign in her rampaging emotions. "I've always thought of the dragon as powerful. As a protector. God knows I need some protection on those streets out there now."

Something in her seemed to snap suddenly. Alex bent, put her head in her hands, and sobbed.

The sight terrified Nikki. Alex never broke down like this. Something must have happened that she didn't know about. Rubbing Alex's back gently, she kissed her temple. "Love, what's wrong? What's happened?"

She was met with silence. She wasn't sure which was worse, Alex yelling or the silence. At least if Alex was shouting Nikki would know what was wrong. Nikki moved her arm up to Alex's shoulders and held her as she sobbed. "Shh…love, talk to me, what's happened?"

A terrible thought occurred to her. "Alex did something happen to Scott?"

Alex shook her head.

Nikki was very worried. "What then, help me to understand - what's going on?"

Alex looked up at her. "I love you, babe, you know that? Oh, Nik…"

Nikki could see the anguish on her face.

Alex noticed the cast still on Nikki's arm. "Your arm, the cast, they didn't take it off…"

"Oh Alex, honey, what happened? I know this isn't about my arm. What's happened?" She held Alex's head between her hands as best she could, and kissed her on the lips. "Tell me please."

"Rachel…."

Nikki controlled her nerves. "Honey, did something happen to the captain's daughter?"

Alex nodded. "She stepped into it at a liquor store. She never saw it coming. God, I hope she didn't. She stopped to get some wine for her date last night. The place was being held up. The guy saw the uniform and panicked. He blew a fucking hole in her. Pete says she died instantly. The shotgun blew a hole the size of a football in her stomach. She didn't stand a chance."

Crying along with her, Nikki held Alex's shaking body. Together they grieved for a lost friend. Seeing her lover sob tore at Nikki's heart.

"They're still out looking for the bastard. May God help him if they bring him back alive, because he'll never make it to trial in one piece. Oh Nikki, you should have seen Mahoney when we told him. It was as if someone tore out his life. He was always so proud of her. His marriage almost broke up because of Rachel becoming a cop. Her mother didn't want her to follow her father's example. God, this fucking sucks! It's not right. She was too young, had too much of a life ahead of her. I could understand if it was me or even Scott. We've been around the block for a long time now. She just got started. Now it's all gone. Her life just extinguished. Fuck!" Alex threw the trowel that was at her feet across the room.

"Don't we have enough problems with some psycho out there taking shots at us without this happening? Shit! Mahoney says if we get another letter or anything unusual, he's going to have to call the FBI. He doesn't want to do that, he wants to keep this internal. Now this…Fuck. How much are we supposed to take?"

Nikki tried to soothe her. She felt the panic rise in her own heart. Someday it could be Alex laying on the ground bleeding to death. She looked down at the tattoo again. Now she understood why Alex felt the need for it. It was defiance against reality.

They sat in silence, neither knew for how long, each drawn back into their own nightmares. Nikki, terrified she would lose Alex in the same way and Alex, afraid once again that she wouldn't be there to protect Nikki. The ring of Alex's cell phone brought them back to the present.

Nikki stood and motioned that she was going downstairs, knowing that Alex needed to talk to Scott in private. Nikki's started to cook dinner. Even if

Alex wasn't hungry, it was something to keep her mind off the vision of Alex lying on the ground bleeding, dying.

†

Later that evening after a subdued dinner, they were relaxing in the living room when it dawned on Alex that Nikki hadn't mentioned how the rest of her interviews went.

Nikki lay on the leather sofa with Alex stretched out between her legs. Nikki gently stroked her fingers through Alex's hair, causing Alex to moan. Reaching up, Alex grasped Nikki's hand and placed a gentle kiss on her palm.

"How were the rest of the interviews? Is there any potential among them?" Alex gently kissed her palm.

"A couple of real losers, one kinda possible, and one probable. I feel somewhat funny about the probable one. She's Mark's niece. I just don't want anyone to say that is why she got the job."

Alex muted the television program they were watching. "Love, no one will think that. Everyone knows you are the fairest person around. They all know you would hire the best person for the job and that that kind of thing doesn't influence you. If she's the best for it, hire her. They'll know that's why she was hired. Have faith in them, the way they do in you. It'll all work out. When did you tell her you'd let her know?"

Alex turned, sliding up so they were lying face to face.

Nikki lifted her head to give Alex a quick kiss on the lips. "I told her I'd let her know on Friday. I just don't know, I guess I worry too much about things. I mean she is the best for the job and seems like a nice person. I think she'd get along with everyone. I really don't think there would be any personality conflicts or anything like that." She smiled at Alex hovering above her. "I know I'm just being a worry-wart."

Alex lowered her head to kiss her and was met halfway. She felt the fire building deep inside her. She needed Nikki, needed the connection it would bring.

"Would you like to *retire to our bedroom*?" Alex wriggled her eyebrows.

In response to Alex's question, Nikki grasped her head, attacking her mouth with her own. She gained entrance into Alex's mouth with her tongue and was lost instantly in the feeling it gave her. "No. Here. Now."

With those words, Alex couldn't hold back. She reached up through the leg of Nikki's boyshorts, finding what she was aching for. Alex drew her fingers through the wetness and was rewarded when she heard Nikki gasp.

Nikki could wait no longer. She felt Alex slowly enter her first with one finger, then two. She wanted more, needed more. Alex pushed up her shirt and found her prize. She greedily sucked on the rigid peak. It was almost more than Nikki could take.

After each slow withdrawal, Alex slowly entered again. She savored each moment of feeling Nikki under her. She straddled Nikki's leg. Nikki came up off the leather couch every time Alex thrust into her. She needed more. Alex could feel the fire building.

It was too much too fast for both of them. Alex had to stop rubbing her center against her. She needed to focus on Nikki.

Nikki needed to come so badly it hurt. Alex wouldn't let her though. Just as she was about to drop over the edge, Alex pulled out of her and whispered in her ear. "Shh, not yet love, not yet. You haven't said please."

Nikki knew by the tone of Alex's voice that her face sported a wicked grin. Alex loved to tease her like this, to bring her to the brink of insanity and leave her there until she begged for release.

She knew what Alex wanted. Nikki gave herself freely. Alex wanted to feel as if she owned her in every sense of the word. Alex needed that control. It was the only thing that made her feel grounded. Nikki also knew the reason for the rough sex. It was Alex's way of releasing the emotions pent up from the previous evening, especially the anger. "Alex please…don't stop."

Nikki pulled Alex's head back to her chest. "Please…" Alex ran her tongue around the hardened nipple, but didn't touch it.

"Alex please, no more teasing."

Alex then switched to the other breast, teasing it in the same fashion. "God, Alex….please!"

Sucking it hard into her mouth, Alex squeezed it at the same time with her free hand. She knew it drove Nikki mad when she did that. Sometimes she could make Nikki come just by that alone.

Today however, Alex needed more. She needed to feel in control. She wanted to hear her scream…to beg. Alex slowly ran her wet fingertips up the inside of Nikki's thigh.

Alex could move like lightning. Nikki never knew it was coming until Alex plunged into her hard. "YES! God, yes!"

Alex thrust harder and faster. "More baby, please." Alex pulled out and added another finger. Nikki could feel the orgasm building. She needed more. She wanted all of Alex inside of her. The couch however was getting too slippery. They wouldn't be able to continue much longer before they slid off onto the floor.

Nikki had to stop Alex so they could move either to the floor or to the bedroom. "Darling stop…hold on. We need to move off the couch. It's getting too slippery. Alex…stop!" She put her hands on Alex's shoulders to push her away from her breast. Alex's eyes were glazed over. "Hon, as much as I love what you're doing we need to move before we fall and one of us gets hurt."

Alex's hand slowly stilled inside of her. She focused on Nikki's face in front of her. Her hand leaving Nikki, she put her fingers up to her mouth and licked each one of them. "Mmm, you taste good. Want a taste?" Alex dipped her fingers back into

Nikki and brought them to her mouth. Nikki licking them drove Alex wild.

Alex watched as Nikki licked the first one slowly, and then greedily sucked them all into her mouth at once. Their eyes met and Alex was lost once more in need.

"Bedroom now…I want you." Alex stood, picked her up, and carried her into the bedroom.

✝

The following morning Nikki groaned as she crawled out of bed, then once again as she sat down behind her desk at work. With their lovemaking spanning into the morning and Alex getting rougher as the night went on, she was more than a little sore. Thankfully, the morning was cool so no one would question the long sleeved turtleneck. She needed it to cover the bruises on her arm and neck, along with the bite marks on her neck. Luckily, her cast ended before her elbow, making it easier to put her clothes on.

Last night was the roughest Alex had ever gotten. They both knew why. It was what Alex needed to deal with Rachel's death. When Nikki left for work, Alex was still asleep. She left her that way, knowing that Alex needed the extra time to try to regroup.

Nikki reset the alarm to eight and sent a text message to Scott telling him that Alex would be a little late that morning. Scott sent a message back telling her he was going to be a little late himself. He had only gotten an hour of sleep.

✝

Nikki sat at her desk sipping coffee, hoping the caffeine would wake her up. She swallowed several aspirin then shifted in her chair to try to get a little more comfortable.

Picking up the phone, she muttered, "Okay first things first, let's call Ms. Scarpella, hire her, and ask her how soon she can start. God, I really hope Alex doesn't freak out. I want this to work out."

Nikki silently hoped Rory Scarpella wouldn't answer, that way she could just leave a message. She lucked out when the voice mail answered. "Ms. Scarpella this is Nikki McLoud regarding the position you interviewed for. I would like to discuss the details with you. Please ring me back either here at the office or on my cell phone. Thanks and I look forward to speaking with you soon."

After hanging up, Nikki remembered she didn't leave her number. "Damn. Well, hopefully she still has my business card."

There was something so disconcerting about the woman that it made her question her decision again. Not able to concentrate on work the rest of the day, her mind kept returning to the striking woman.

The return call came later that night as she was taking out the garbage. Usually Alex took it to the curb, however, she was still at the station with Scott. Having very little to go on, they had yet to find the shooter. Nikki had eaten a small salad to tide her over until Alex got home. As she came back into the house, her cell phone rang.

"Hello, Nikki McLoud." Her heart skipped a beat when she heard the voice.

"Hi, this is Rory. I'm returning your phone call. I really hope this means I am being considered for the position."

There was a long pause as Nikki found her train of thought. "Actually, Ms. Scarpella, I wanted to discuss when you would be able to start." Nikki chuckled. "So, yes I guess you could say you're being considered for the position."

"Please call me Rory. I can start next Monday if you like. As I said yesterday, I'm free to start whenever you would like. Monday though would give me time to get some boxes unpacked."

Nikki heard the excitement in Rory's voice.

✝

She really wanted this job for more than one reason, some of which she would keep to herself. One of the reasons being she wanted to prove that she was not the black sheep of the family, nor the total screw-up they thought her to be.

One way or another she would prove to them that she had what it took to do the job. Meeting her girlfriend, Lydia, had, in some ways, helped her along that path. In others, it made things worse. Some members of her family were very bigoted, while others couldn't have cared less. Those that didn't hate her for being gay didn't want her around because of the crowd she hung around with in her youth.

When she was young, the police made numerous trips to Rory's parents' home with her in tow. When she was very young, the police would return her with just a warning. As she got older, the charges became worse and they started to stick with her. Then she barely graduated high school. After graduation, Rory worked for her uncle's landscaping business. Her family hoped that would keep her out of trouble but that was not to be the case.

For the first year, everything went well until she got bored. Once again, Rory started hanging out with old friends. The final straw with her parents came when the police called them at three in the morning on a Saturday to tell them that their daughter had been arrested for being involved in an armed robbery. She spent six months in jail. All of this had been most embarrassing for her father, to say the least, considering he was a homicide detective.

Since that day, she had been trying to prove herself. She needed them to be proud of her, to believe in her.

Plus, she hated to admit it. Something about Nikki pulled at her. She couldn't figure out what it was, only that she saw deep pain in Nikki's eyes.

"Um, Monday will be fine. If you want to stop by the office for the paperwork before that just let me know. If you do so, I'll already have you in the system and your badge will be ready to go first thing in the morning." Nikki prayed she would say no. She didn't want to take the chance that Rory would see anything she shouldn't.

"That would be great. I'll run by first thing in the morning. I then want to go to the mall to pick up a few items. It's quite handy to have the mall practically next door, especially since I finally just moved in yesterday and need quite a few items."

†

Nikki's heart rate doubled. She knew she had no right to ask, but she had to. Her curiosity wouldn't let her keep her mouth shut. Nikki was unsure where Rory lived because her resume had her old address on it.

"Which mall?" Nikki held her breath.

"It's called Eastview Mall. This place has everything, plus it's easy to get in and out of. I really hate shopping. I always know what I want before I go, so I just go in, get what I want and leave. Do you live close to it?" Rory was greeted with silence.

"Which street exactly do you live on?" Nikki asked quietly. Her head started to pound, knowing what the answer would be.

Nikki remembered seeing a house for sale on the next street but there were no signs of someone living there. She panicked. She almost dropped the phone when she heard the address. It indeed was the house around the corner.

†

Rory noticed she was once again greeted with silence. "Nikki?" She wondered if there was something wrong with her new employer.

"Actually you live right around the corner. My back yard overlooks the winery. So ah, Rory, I guess I'll see you in the morning. I need to finish some things before I relax for the night."

Rory tried to think of something to keep the conversation going. "I guess I should go too, I've kept you on the phone for quite a while. It's late, I haven't eaten dinner yet, and I'm starving for Italian. Where is the best place to go around here?"

As an afterthought she added, "Have you eaten dinner yet?" Rory didn't know why she asked. It just slipped out.

✝

Nikki thought for a moment. "The best place I know of is at the mall, in the new front section. As for the other, I had a salad when I got home. Thank you for asking though. I really need to get going. I have work to get done this evening. Bye."

When she hung up, Nikki had to wipe her sweaty palms on her shorts. There was something so familiar about this woman. She couldn't believe it. This was not a good thing. It was a bad thing, a very bad thing, indeed.

✝

An hour later, Nikki sat at the table putting the finishing touches on her budget for the next quarter when the doorbell rang. "Who the hell can that be?"

Then her mind turned another corner. "Oh God, something's happened to Alex."

She threw her pen onto the table and ran down the hall to the front door.

Nikki yanked the door open. "Alex…" There before her stood Rory, holding what looked like a take-out bag.

✝

Rory stood rooted to the spot gaping at the stunning vision before her. Nikki wore shorts and a tank top that had only thin spaghetti straps holding it up. That mouth-watering sight alone was enough to make Rory's heart race.

Then her eyes strayed to the tattoo on her arm. She found the tattoo interesting, not expecting a woman like Nikki to have one. Then she saw them. Rory felt the anger rise in her. Anger like she had never known before. Rory stared at the bruises and bite mark.

Rory started to comment but stopped herself. It was none of her business, not really. Yet something told her to make it her business, to protect this woman. "Nikki…"

✝

Nikki felt Rory's eyes travel across her body. She knew where her eyes landed. It wasn't on her tattoo or on her large breasts. They settled on what she wanted to conceal the most. Nikki watched as Rory's emotions played close to the surface.

The only way out of the situation was to pretend she didn't know where Rory's eyes were fixated. A chill swept through Nikki, causing goose bumps to break out on her arms.

"Rory what are you doing here?"

"Dinner?" Rory held up the shopping bag.

"I, um, well…why don't you come in? It seems to be getting cooler, let me just throw on a shirt. Why don't you go on through to the kitchen and I'll meet you there?"

Turning to the staircase to make a quick exit, Nikki pointed in the direction of the kitchen.

Panicked, Nikki raced to the bedroom. "This is bad. If Alex comes home and finds Rory here, especially with dinner, she'll lose it right on the spot. She'll blow like a volcano."

Nikki knew she had to get Rory out of there as fast as possible without making it too obvious. Throwing on a long sleeve T-shirt Nikki raced back to the kitchen.

"Sorry it took me so long. What brings you here?" Nikki leaned against the island as Rory started to unpack the food she'd brought.

Rory paused for a moment, "You need more than just a salad, I was starving, and I hate eating alone. So here I am. I thought I might as well do the paperwork tonight also. That is if you happen to have it on-line."

Nikki looked around the kitchen, her eyes settling on the phone. She could just call Alex to see how long she was going to be. That way she would know how long she had to get Rory out of there, or she could try another approach. She stood by the island in the middle of the kitchen twisting the ring on her finger.

†

Noticing the nervousness, Rory thought she was causing it. Thoughts raced through her mind. Nikki was not a lesbian like she had thought. That Nikki was actually homophobic and had found out that Rory was a lesbian. It then hit Rory. Alex was a guy.

Rory stood up ready to bolt from the house. She was afraid to know the true answer. For a reason she couldn't fathom she didn't want to find out it was a man. She wanted to keep the hope alive in her heart that it was a woman. That revelation alone wanted to make her run all the more.

Rory froze. She couldn't do this. Yet, she looked at Nikki out of the corner of her eye. Nikki was so damn good looking but it was more than that. She watched Nikki raise her head and heard her gasp when their eyes met. Both felt the thread of connection.

†

Nikki opened her mouth to say no. What came out was, "Yes."

Rory's dark eyebrow shot up. She repeated Nikki's words. "Yes?"

The trance was broken when she felt Rory's hand on her arm. She had to regain her composure fast so that Rory wouldn't think she was coming to work for a flake. "Yes, uh, yes I would love something to eat. Let me get some plates. Would you like a glass of wine?"

†

Rory finished unpacking the dinners. "Yes, that would be nice, but only if you are going to have some. Don't open a bottle just for me. I hope you like chicken and shrimp dishes. I got one of each with a couple of dishes of pasta."

She watched as Nikki tried to reach the wine glasses on a shelf that was way too high for her. Stepping behind her, Rory reached the shelf easily. Setting the glasses on the counter, she realized she had unconsciously put her left hand on Nikki's shoulder. Leaning above Nikki slightly she could easily whisper into Nikki's ear.

Rory could feel the heat coming off the smaller woman's body in waves. "Mm, you smell good. What perfume is that?" Rory couldn't help herself. She sniffed Nikki's neck.

†

Nikki froze. What if Alex walked in? What if she didn't? She stepped away from Rory. "It's Black by Kenneth Cole." Then without even thinking she added, "Its Alex's favorite." At those words, she saw a flicker of sadness wash across Rory's face.

They ate while Nikki filled Rory in on what would be required of her. She also told her about the project that was starting on Monday. After Rory shared some about herself and what ideas she could contribute, they discussed exactly what Nikki did. Not once did either ask the other anything personal.

Before they realized it, three hours had passed, all the while one question still burned in Rory's mind. Finally, she had to ask it, no matter what the outcome.

While Nikki was pouring them another cup of coffee, Rory's question came unexpectedly. It startled Nikki.

"Nikki, if you don't mind me asking, what exactly does Alex do for a living? When you came to the door, you looked a little worried. Is his job dangerous or is it something else?" Sitting on the sofa, she sipped her coffee. Rory watched Nikki smile, then chuckle.

"Ah, Rory I think there is something you should know. Alex is—" The ringing phone interrupted Nikki.

Nikki knew without answering who it was. She could feel it. Her stomach flipped and she felt nauseous. "Excuse me while I get that." Hitting the answer button, she walked into the kitchen. "Hello?"

It was indeed Alex. She sounded tired and miserable. Nikki sighed in relief when Alex told her she was going to be another couple of hours. Nikki watched as Rory walked into the kitchen and set the cups into the sink.

Alex heard the dishes clanking in the background. "I thought you were going to wait to eat when I got home?"

Without turning around Rory called to Nikki to tell her she was going to head out and that she would see her on Monday.

It was too late to cover the mouthpiece on the phone. Alex had heard her. Rory saw the stricken look on Nikki's face.

"Uh, Alex…" She held the phone away from her ear as Alex went off on a tirade.

Rory could hear Alex's shouting across the room. Her mouth dropped open in shock.

Nikki's eyes met hers and pleaded to her- please don't.

Deciding to stay after all, Rory pointed at the living room and walked away.

"Alex, please calm down. Remember I hired Rory. Well I thought it would be a good idea to go over all the paperwork tonight so she could just jump into work on Monday. Yes, I'm waiting to eat when you come home. We just had coffee and I was just putting our coffee cups into the sink. Now please tell me what you were going to say." Nikki hadn't realized until that moment that tears were running down her face. She knew she would more than likely pay later. Nikki thought about how nice the dinner with Rory had been and she smiled.

Rory stood in the living room trying hard not to eavesdrop. Her mind raced. Alex was a woman. She pumped her fist in the air in joy and mouthed *yes*. Then just as quickly, she wondered why Nikki lied to Alex about dinner.

What outraged her though was Alex's language. That and she sounded like she was accusing Nikki of something. Rory disliked the woman already and she had yet to meet her. When Nikki came into the room, Rory stopped in her tracks, realizing she had been pacing.

Nikki looked up at her, tried to say something then stopped. Rory could tell she was gathering her thoughts so she gave her a moment.

"As I was going to say before the phone rang, Alex is a woman." Nikki then did something she hadn't done in years. She blushed. "Do you have a moment to talk some more or do you have to be going?"

Nikki motioned to the couch. They both sat, Nikki in Alex's La-Z-Boy™ and Rory on the leather couch.

"Alex is a homicide lieutenant and they're working a big case right now. She called to say she won't be home for a couple more hours. If you'd like we could talk some more, if you're not too tired."

Nikki didn't know why but she suddenly felt shy. She wanted this woman to like her. What she didn't want was Alex messing it up. It was bad enough that Alex and Liz didn't get along. Not feeling comfortable around Alex, she and Nikki usually went shopping or to lunch when Alex was at work.

Rory knew she shouldn't ask but she was curious. "What case are they working on? Is it anything that's been on the news?" Kicking off her shoes, she gathered her feet up under her while she waited for Nikki to answer.

Nikki watched her get comfortable, startled at how at comfortable she looked. She looked like she belonged in Nikki's home….their home. Nikki knew she had to get her thoughts in check. Damn why did Rory have to be so striking? Worse yet though, why did she feel this connection to her?

"Um, they are still looking for the guy that killed Rachel. She was their captain's daughter and a fellow police officer. It's kind of made all of them on edge, angry and jumpy. She and Scott have been putting in long hours every day. And then there are the letters Alex has received during the past few weeks."

Rory could see the sadness and loneliness in Nikki's eyes. She also saw something else—fear.

Nikki flinched inwardly. Why had she told her about the letters? Alex would have a meltdown if she found out. For reasons unknown to Nikki, the words just tumbled out one after another.

✝

Rory moved from the couch to kneel in front of Nikki. Taking Nikki's hands, she looked at the cast on her arm. Rory felt the anger flame once again in the pit of her stomach. She made a conscious decision to go out on a limb. This woman needed her. Rory knew it deep in her soul.

"Nikki, I know we don't know one another, but if you need to talk, I have good ears. I know a little something about cops. My father was one. He was a homicide detective. He was killed three years ago by a ten-year-old gang-banger. I know, for instance that they work 'til they drop from exhaustion. I also know they can sometimes have foul tempers." She looked down at their intertwined hands.

"I also dated one for a couple of months. She had a temper to match all tempers and damn did she like…" Rory looked up into Nikki's eyes, squeezing her hands.

"She liked rough sex. She actually craved it. Now don't get me wrong, I like things kind of wild sometimes, but not brutal like she did. During those six months we were together I was in the emergency room twice."

She ran her fingertip along Nikki's jaw line. "If you ever need anything, do not hesitate to call, especially with her receiving threats. Don't take any chances, please."

"Alex loves me. She is kind, gentle, and one of the most loving people I know. She would never hurt me. I know what you mean about being wound tight sometimes though. This case has them all tied in knots. None of them are getting any sleep or relaxation and it's starting to take its toll on them.

Alex works off her frustration by doing projects around the house. Would you like to see one of her projects?"

Nikki tried to steer them off the subject of Alex's temper. If Alex knew they were having this conversation, there would be hell to pay.

She tried hard to convince Rory that Alex was a good person and not capable of the brutality that Rory described. In a way, she was also trying to convince herself. Nikki knew Alex never meant to hurt her, not really. She just couldn't control herself sometimes and things happened. Nikki showed her around the house, saving Alex's bathroom project for last.

Rory looked around the room in awe. "She really did this? Wow, it's wonderful. She's quite talented. May I look around in more detail?" Nikki nodded and Rory studied the room.

"This is just amazing. Do you think she'd consider remodeling a couple rooms in my house? I'm sure she'll need to work off some more tension. Do you think I could ask her?" Rory was crouching and looking at the ceramic tile on the floor.

"Of course you can. I'm sure she'd be flattered if you asked. Why don't we arrange dinner sometime this week?" Nikki had been leaning in the doorway watching her when Rory stood and walked toward her.

"So Nikki, what kind of talents do you have? I am sure quite a few."

Nikki thought for a moment then, shook her head. "Sorry, nope. Alex has all the talent. I'm pretty much just, well…I can cook." Nikki walked away down the hall, not realizing she was talking aloud. "Just useless otherwise…"

Rory was stunned by what she heard, hoping she had heard her incorrectly. She put her hands on Nikki's shoulders to turn her around. "What did you say?"

Nikki looked horrified that she'd spoken aloud. "Nothing…It was nothing."

As they walked down the steps, Alex walked in the front door. The scowl on her face told Nikki she was in a foul mood. Before the situation got out of hand, she tried to diffuse it. "Alex this is Rory. Rory, I would like you to meet Alex."

Alex shook Rory's hand hard. "Hello, I'm Alex. Nikki's wife. It's very nice to meet you. I'd like to thank you for keeping her company tonight. I'm sure it gets lonely for her sometimes."

Rory noticed Alex put her arm around Nikki's waist, squeezing tight. She thought it best to change the subject.

"I was admiring your work around the house. You are quite skilled, my compliments. I was just mentioning to Nikki that I was going to ask you if you would like to do some work for me. I have a couple of rooms that are in need of some major renovating. I especially love the tile and the glass block shower in the one bathroom."

✝

Alex looked down at Nikki. She knew that Rory would've had to go through their bedroom to see the bathroom she was talking about. She was not in the mindset to entertain tonight. To top it off she was pissed at Nikki for letting anyone into their bedroom when she wasn't there. Alex wondered what else the woman was doing in their bedroom.

An evil grin spread across Alex's face. She was going to have a little fun at their expense. The other two women saw the look. One was terrified of the look, the other begging her to do something stupid, so she could kick the shit out of her.

Alex grasped Nikki's left breast. "So did Nikki also show you our bedroom? We originally had a queen size bed, but I decided we needed a king size. You know how it is. Those smaller beds are sometimes just not big enough to play *reindeer games* in."

Alex knew she'd hit on something when she saw Nikki blush and tense up. She then watched as Rory took more of a defensive stand.

Wanting to push Rory into making a mistake, Alex egged her on. "I also made the sleigh bed frame. I made it out of ash wood, one of the hardest woods. I wanted it to be sturdy. I hate it when the wood on a headboard splinters from overuse, don't you?"

Alex looked directly into Rory's eyes, challenging her.

Rory wasn't about to back down. "Yes, that is such a bitch when that happens, especially when metal rubs against the wood of an un-sturdy headboard. So, do you think you would be interested?"

"Love to, let me know when you want me to look at the rooms. Were you just on your way out then?" Alex moved to open the front door.

†

Rory looked at Nikki and saw nothing there, absolutely nothing. That made her even more worried about Nikki. Rory wondered if that was how she coped. If she just shut off everything inside.

"Yes, I guess I was. I'll call you about the rooms once I get settled in. Nikki, thank you for making me feel welcome in a new community. I guess I'll see you on Monday then." She turned as if to leave and hesitated.

She turned back to Alex, deciding to get in one last jab. "Do you happen to know of a good dojo around here? I already have several black belts and was training to be a master in Kendo."

†

Alex contemplated it for a moment. Was Rory threatening her? Was Rory saying she could handle herself and to watch out? Alex's eyes narrowed and Rory knew the woman caught her meaning. "I'll ask around the station and let you know."

Alex closed the door then turned toward Nikki and glared. "So did you have a good evening?"

Nikki was obviously afraid. "Do you want me to start dinner, sweetie?"

Alex whispered in her ear. "No." She ripped off Nikki's shirt and threw it across the room. "You belong to me."

Nikki inwardly sighed. She just had to relax and breathe. It would be done soon. She prayed that it wouldn't go on for hours like it sometimes did when Alex was angry.

Sometime later, she looked down. She remembered. Good screaming, then an overturned table. A broken vase, then more good screaming. Bad screaming as Alex carved an 'A' with a piece of the vase into her skin, above her pubic hairline. Then blood.

The only word heard from Alex the whole time was one word repeated again and again— "Mine." And lastly she remembered hearing Alex's cell phone ringing in the background. Nikki listened to her yell *yes*, when Scott gave her the news that they had found Rachel's killer.

When Alex went to the den to answer her phone, Nikki looked at the shambles of the living room. As she picked up the mess, she chastised herself. She muttered as she cleaned. "Oh Rory, if only you could help me. I've lost hope. Now it's just a matter of helping Alex through this because she needs me."

Chapter Two

Hades Hath No Fury

Two torturous months had passed since that night; or eight weeks; or sixty-one days; or two thousand four hundred forty hours; or one hundred twenty-two thousand four hundred minutes. Whichever way you calculated it every single one of those minutes was pure anguish for Captain William Mahoney.

He was a good cop. Every officer knew it. Not one of them could blame him for what he had done. His rapport with the community was above reproach. He loved his daughters. Rachel though, she had been his pride and joy, his heir. He had visions of her one day sitting in his chair after he'd retired. He would then be living the high life, sitting in his living room bouncing Rachel and her girlfriend's children on his knees. Now none of that would be happening. It was all gone. It had only taken a split second, a pull of the trigger and a future ceased.

Mahoney continued to pace in his office, as he had been doing for more than an hour. He wasn't sure how much longer it would be his office if they didn't find the man guilty. It was bad enough they wouldn't let him anywhere near the courthouse, but knowing that the verdict was supposed to have come in more than twenty minutes ago and no one had called him was killing him.

Even though not a thing could be proven, the attorney for the defendant obtained a restraining order against the captain. Because of that order, he couldn't attend the trial. The incident stemmed back to the night when they brought in the suspect for Rachel's killing.

The suspect was a lowly peon in one of the local gangs, even though he had a rap sheet of violent crimes a mile long. Trying to move up in status, he had boasted of killing the young female cop. As if he was tired of doing all the dirty work, yet receiving none of the credit.

The gang he ran with was already in deep trouble in other matters. They didn't need a cop killer amongst their ranks. Unbeknownst to the rest of the gang, the leader and his second in command tied the kid up like a Christmas package. They then called the station and told them where to pick up their killer. They acted as though they had no problems with killing other gang members, but the death of a cop brought way too much dirt to their doorsteps.

After Scott removed the duct tape from his mouth, the kid decided not to wait for his lawyer. He admitted to the robbery and killing the cop. Once his lawyer arrived, they tried to plea bargain. However, the DA would have none of that. A trial date was set, with the young man held without bail. The kid never squawked once, he knew he was safer in jail.

When they brought the suspect to the interrogation room in the basement, Mahoney had been there waiting. The officers would have to go through the side door and down the steps in order to get to the basement. He took the kid by the handcuffs then proceeded to drag him roughly down the steps, making sure several of the steps came up to greet him on the way down. The three officers accompanying them testified that he was already beaten up when they found him dressed like a Thanksgiving turkey. Even though nothing could be proven, the restraining order was issued.

The Captain was also worried about Alex. There had been two more nasty-grams in the past few weeks.

He stopped his pacing in front of his large window that overlooked the main station area. All the desks sat in straight rows, cluttered with days of paperwork. Every detective in the station had been too busy with the trial to care about such tedious things. The filing would be there for them to finish when Rachel's killer was behind bars for good.

Mahoney rubbed his temples.

"We don't have long before the FBI steps in. I've been lucky to hold them off this long."

The shrill ringing of his cell phone rudely interrupted his musings. He quickly answered it.

It was Scott. The verdict was declared. They found his daughter's killer guilty. Since he had so many violent priors, Mahoney hoped the man would receive life in prison with no parole for killing a cop. Even though that would be too good for the murderer.

Living in general was too good for him because no matter what, Rachel couldn't be brought back. He wanted the man dead—an eye for an eye, a life for a life. The Captain grew angrier by the day. Now he had no one to go home to talk about it with since his wife had left him five weeks earlier. The rift that grew between he and his wife became too great for her to bear. She blamed him for their daughter's death, only adding to the tremendous guilt he already faced with holding himself responsible for not being able to protect her.

The only thing that kept him going was that he knew Scott and Alex needed him. They needed his leadership and years of experience to find the bastard that, just that morning, had left Nikki a dozen black roses with a sympathy card for the demise of Alex. Also in the box was a pair of black lacy panties that smelled like Alex's cologne and a rather personal note addressed to Nikki herself.

The note stated that the sender knew that they were a favorite pair of Nikki's. It also said that they knew she was bare down there. Whoever was doing this went a step further this time. They ended the letter with *I know Alex demands you keep your pussy shaved clean.* The gifts were bad enough but the note was what almost sent Nikki over the edge. She was terrified to go anywhere alone, not knowing what was going to happen.

The panties scared her. They were an exact match for a pair that she owned. When Nikki saw them, she ran to their bedroom to make sure hers were still in her drawer. She then called the captain, knowing that Alex and Scott were in the courtroom. He sent two officers over, one to pick up the box and bring it back to the office. The other was to remain with her until Alex got home.

Before he hung up with Scott, he explained what had happened that morning. Scott's anxiety skyrocketed as he listened, his thoughts going to his wife and daughter. It would kill him if anything happened like this to her. Whoever was doing this knew Alex personally.

†

Just as he thought would happen, Alex went ballistic, demanding Scott drive her home right then.

"So help me Scott, if that bastard touches one hair on her head I'll kill him. I don't care if he comes after me—let him. I'll tear him apart with my bare hands. Shit, Scott, who can it be? It's obvious it's nobody we've previously arrested. None of them were this personal. None of them knew the things in those letters. I just don't fucking get it."

She pounded her fists on the dashboard as he drove.

"I know what you mean, Alex. The things in those letters— it has to be someone who knows the two of you well. I agree he's one sick bastard. Alex, I have to ask you a very personal question. I know we're close, but this is really personal. Okay?"

Alex contemplated his question. Yes, they were close, yes, they talked about everything, but there were some things that you didn't even talk to your best friend about. She knew what he was going

57

to ask. It was going to be a doozy of a conversation. She nodded her head. "Shoot."

Scott swallowed the lump in his throat, knowing his face was turning red. "It was one of the things in the last letter." His courage faltered.

Alex chuckled. "Which one, there were so many in that lovely letter." She watched out the window as Scott pulled off into an empty parking lot. He sighed, shutting off the engine.

Any time he pulled over, it was always one of their long philosophical discussions.

"Scott, which one would that be? The one where it says I'm into S&M or the one where I'm into animals? 'Cause the animal one is just gross and one hundred percent not true."

He turned to Alex. "So the S&M one is? Damn woman. Did you really do those things? Shit!"

Alex leaned forward, banging her head on the dashboard.

Raising up and looking him in the eyes, Alex explained while trying not to shock him. "Scott, we're best friends so I won't lie or try hide the truth. That's one thing I've always promised you that I would never do. Shit, where to start? Okay, yes, I used to go to leather bars when I was younger. I haven't been to them in years and I do mean years. I think the last time I was in one was when I was twenty-five. Did I fuck some woman with a beer bottle right in the middle of the bar so that everyone could see us the last time I was in one? Yes, I did. As I said, I was wild back then. I thought it was the only way I could feel anything sometimes. Did I do the rest of it?"

Alex paused, knowing she was about to give him either a heart attack or a hard-on or worse. He could arrest her. "Yes, she was so weak after I did that to her that she had fallen to her knees. I then grabbed her by her nipples, pulled her up and threw her onto a table. I then flipped her and proceeded to fuck her up the ass with the handle of a whip someone had handed me. That is, after I hit her across the ass several times with it.

"And yes, two other women held her down while I did this, and yes she was begging for us to stop. I, however, at that point was not really in my body if you know what I mean. There was this blonde that had eyes on me all night and I finally gave into her. I let her pull my leather pants down and go down on me while I was helping myself to the redhead that was being held down. Then while I had been fucking the other up the ass with the whip, blondie picked up the bottle and used it on me. So you can truly understand why I was out of my mind.

"I'm not proud of any of it, Scott, but I won't deny any of it. I did it all, every last disgusting item on the list, except the animal shit. I just hope you don't think any less of me, that this doesn't change our friendship." She looked him in the eyes.

Alex was shocked and Alex fully expected to see hatred and disgust there. What she saw was warmth, kindness, and understanding. Scott had been her friend since day one. His understanding told her he would remain so through to the end.

Scott coughed then laughed. "Well, I guess I asked. Shit, woman, so… is it really true that you have a tattoo and piercing down there?" He grinned, thinking he'd finally gotten her goat.

"Scott…" She buried her face in her hands. For the first time, she felt humility at all she had done. Sure, she had done those things, but every single person makes mistakes and she herself was only human.

"Yes, Alex?" He gave a perfect smile, the kind that says, make my day, please.

She saw the smile and decided two could play that game. Yes, two could play that game. Should she make his day? Alex knew Tessa would approve, knowing he deserved what he had coming to him.

Alex lifted her head, meeting his eyes once more.

What Scott saw in them this time made him regret his last question. He was going to be treated to her wicked side, he just knew it, and he knew he deserved it.

Alex put her hand on his thigh. Leaning she purred into his ear. "Actually, Scott, yes, it's true. Would you like to see? The tattoo is a lollipop. The stick of it leads right to my clit where the ring is. So, would you like to see? Or maybe you'd like to see the ring through my left nipple? It matches the one down there. Hmm Scott?"

The look on his face said it all. He was sweating bullets. "Damn it, Alex... I think I need to get you home to Nikki so I can get home to Tessa.

Damn, woman, you've corrupted me over the years. For some reason none of this shocks me anymore."

He gave a full belly laugh, which in turn made Alex roar with laughter. "Lady, is there nothing you haven't done? Wait, don't answer that! Shit, I need to get home."

Starting the truck, he then had her home in record time. On the way, they discussed who possibly could know so many personal details. Scott then asked the question that had been on his mind for a couple of months now. "Alex, question. Could this be a woman? Maybe someone you've slept with? Someone we haven't talked to yet? I know we've talked to everyone we thought had any connections to the letters. But maybe we're missing someone."

Alex thought about it a moment. Who could it be? Who was demented enough to be doing this? "No, I don't think it's a woman Scott. This is just so fucked-up. Whoever it is, is watching us. I mean *really* watching us."

They finally pulled into Alex's driveway and saw an extra vehicle there. Both knew who it belonged to. Scott knew firsthand that Alex neither liked the woman, nor trusted her, thinking Rory and Nikki had become too chummy.

"Fuck! I am so not in the mood for this today. I thought Mahoney said he left a uniform here. Where the hell is the car?" Fury coursed through Alex. If her girlfriend needed to be comforted or protected she, Alex, would be the one to do it, not some butch who thought she was Nikki's savior.

†

In between calling the captain about the box and the arrival of the two officers, Nikki received another call. She hadn't even had enough time to call her boss Mark to let him know that she wouldn't be in to work. Mark and his wife Janet were two of only a handful of people who knew that Nikki was being threatened.

Mahoney had asked everyone to keep it as quiet as possible which meant no one else knowing. Mark, however, had to be informed since several times Nikki had been too upset to work. He also had to be informed since they were investigating all angles, including if it was someone she worked with.

When Nikki's cell phone rang, it startled her and she dropped it to the hardwood floor. She checked the caller ID. The display read her direct office line number. *Who could be calling from her personal office?*

"Hello?" She answered timidly.

Her hand shook when she heard the voice. Why did it have such an effect on her?

"Nikki? Are you there? Is everything okay? Nikki?" Rory's voice broke through the haze.

"Sorry Rory, it has, uh, not been a great morning. Is everything okay there?"

Nikki desperately needed someone to confide in. She couldn't talk to Liz about it. Her friend already didn't like Alex and she most assuredly would somehow make this Alex's fault. The two of them couldn't be civil to one another for more than five minutes as a time. On the other hand, Alex really didn't like Rory either.

Her mind turned back to Rory. Could she completely trust this woman? Nikki didn't know why, but she did trust her. Something drew her to Rory. However, could she trust her without reservation? Nikki knew the answer to that without any hesitation. Yes, she could trust Rory with her life, even knowing she could not fully open up to her.

"Yes, everything is fine here. I was just worried about you. We were supposed to work on the Cheese Project today and it's not like you not to show up when there is a project due. I've only known you for a short time, but I can tell something isn't right here. So I decided to come into your office for some privacy while I called you. Nikki, you know you can talk to me."

†

Rory waited, giving her time. She was positive it had to do with Alex.

Rory only hoped Alex hadn't beaten Nikki again. Even though Nikki would never admit it, Rory knew. She knew in the pit of her stomach that Alex was an abuser. What she couldn't figure out, for the life of her, was why Nikki would put up with it.

Suddenly Rory heard sobbing through the phone.

"Nikki, I'm on my way. Just hang on." Slamming the phone down Rory ran from the office.

Rory warred with herself as she drove. *She's such a beautiful woman. She's also extremely intelligent, funny, thoughtful, caring... I can't understand why she's with someone like Alex. I'm sure she broke Nikki's arm, just as I'm sure she's responsible for the bruises too. So help me I'll fucking kill the bitch if she's hurt her. I'll snap her head like a fucking twig. So help me God, I'll do it.*

Rory ignored the speed limits, praying there were no cops. She didn't even want to think about what she'd done to Nikki before this. Had Alex broken other bones, beaten her, or worse? The *or worse* sent fury coursing through her veins.

Rory gasped. "Damn! All I had to do is look at Alex and I know what she's capable of." Was Alex capable of the ultimate betrayal of her girlfriend's body and soul? Yes, she knew she was. If Rory ever found out that the bitch had forced herself on Nikki...Rory smiled suddenly. She wouldn't like meeting an old friend of hers.

Rory couldn't accuse Alex of spousal abuse without proof. She valued Nikki's friendship and wanted to protect her. By the Gods, she liked her, more than she should.

She was torn. Nikki was with Alex and she herself had a girlfriend who was due to arrive any day. Her nights were spent either lying in bed fantasizing about Nikki or going to the club for relief. She had never been drawn to anyone like she was to Nikki. She was damn glad that her girlfriend Lydia would be there soon.

When Rory arrived at Nikki's house, her heart stopped. In the driveway were two patrol cars, but their lights were not flashing. She thought the worst. *Oh God, I'm too late…*

Shutting off the engine, she ran from the car, not even bothering to worry whether the car door closed or not. She didn't even consider taking the extra second to set the locks or alarm. Rory's mind told her Nikki needed her. That was all that mattered.

A uniformed officer stopped her at the door, asking for identification. Nikki heard Rory demanding loudly to be let in, that she was Nikki's friend.

"It's okay, officer, I asked her to come here."

The officer turned to Nikki as she approached him. "Ma'am I was informed not to let anyone in until Lt. Canton or Detective Jackson get here."

Nikki addressed him one on one. "Officer, I said I asked her to come here. I will not be told what to do in my own home. Please take the box and its contents and leave. Ms. Scarpella will be here with me. She holds several different black belts—no one would want to tangle with her."

The second officer pulled him aside before the naive officer could open his mouth again. He'd seen the woman at the local gym and the gun club. "She'll be in good hands and personally, that woman scares me," he whispered.

"As I said this is my home. You have what you came for. I would like you to take it to Captain Mahoney. Now please leave."

Knowing they couldn't stay after being asked to leave, they picked up the evidence bag and departed. Nikki closed the door behind them, resting her head on it. Her body started to shake again. She felt Rory put her arm around her waist. The taller woman then led her into the living room to sit down.

Rory grabbed the box of tissues and sat beside her. She wiped the tears from Nikki's face. "Sweetie, tell me what's going on. Is it something with Alex? Has she done something?"

Nikki tried to stop the crying but only succeeded in hyperventilating. She felt the other woman's warm hand on her back rubbing circles on it, while the other caressed her face.

"Shh, it's okay. Whatever it is, it'll be okay. When you can, tell me what's going on."

Nikki relaxed into Rory's touch. She wasn't sure where to start. There was no way she could tell her all of it. Nikki only dared to tell her the edited version. She told her about one of the letters, the calls, but not about the box she had received that day.

She left out the exact details of some of the items. Yes, they had become close and they talked about personal things, but some of the topics embarrassed her. On top of that, Nikki didn't want anyone to know about several of the items in the letters to Alex.

Nikki was terrified to verbalize that Alex was capable of some of those things. When she read the letters, they left her speechless. Nikki could only imagine how others would react. She worried what

Rory's reaction would be. She didn't want Alex to hurt Rory, if the two were to clash.

Rory heard more than Nikki realized. That told her there were details Nikki left out. What was Nikki afraid of? Was Nikki afraid of her judging her or Alex, or was she embarrassed? They had become friends, but, Nikki didn't trust her completely.

Rory's words must have been written on her face, because Nikki answered several of her silent questions.

"I…uh…left some of the more extremely personal things out. One or two of them are a little embarrassing." Nikki's face turned crimson.

"Nikki, you can tell me anything, don't ever forget that. I'll never judge you. We've talked about some pretty racy stuff before this. Please don't feel embarrassed. Let me go make you some tea, okay?"

"Okay. Thanks."

Sipping her tea, Nikki thought about what Rory said. Did she trust the other woman enough? No, not for the big thing, but enough to tell Rory more. She had yet to tell her about the box she had just received. Deciding to trust Rory, Nikki first told her about the letter that Alex had received two weeks ago. It caused Rory to flip out.

Nikki wasn't sure what freaked Rory out more, the piercings Alex had, the whip that was in the box, or what was in the letter. After hearing about the letter, Rory stood, walked to the kitchen, and returned with a beer in her hand. By the time she'd walked back into the living room, half the beer was gone.

Rory sat beside her once more and took another long drink from the beer. Nikki was ready to open up more, but she did nothing to push her. Rory wanted her to take her time, to let it come gradually.

Nikki turned on the couch, pulling her legs up to her chest. "This morning's package was aimed at me. It seems whoever is doing this is now focusing on me. I'm just so…I don't know how to say this—it's just that it's so private."

Nikki hesitated, picked up her tea, and sipped it. Trying to stall for time, she contemplated the correct words. Nikki didn't want it coming out too crude. "In the box were a dozen black roses and a sympathy card to me, sending me their sympathy for Alex's death."

"Was there more in the box?" She knew there was. Nikki was too upset for there not to have been.

The tears fell once more. "Yes, there was a letter addressed to me and a couple of personal items. Oh, God… There was a pair of black lace panties."

Rory was puzzled. "Nikki, millions of women own black lace panties. Was there something special about them?" Rory held her breath.

Nikki lowered her head and blushed. "They were crotchless and identical to mine."

She pictured Nikki wearing the dainty lace panties and was instantly wet. She had to refocus her attention. "Okay…and?"

Still embarrassed, Nikki continued. "They smelled just like Alex's cologne. I raced upstairs, but mine were still in the drawer. There was also a…ah…a…" Nikki looked down at her shaking hands. She watched Rory's hands reach and hold hers.

Nikki couldn't comprehend why, but she found comfort in Rory holding her hands. That thought frightened her. She was in love with Alex, how could she feel comforted by another woman? Looking up, their eyes met.

In those eyes, the color of blue ice, she saw anger. Nikki knew it wasn't directed at her. For an unexplained reason it calmed her knowing Rory cared. Taking a deep cleansing breath, she continued.

"There was also a shaver. Let's just say the kind that you use to shave when you want to wear a bikini. In the letter, there were some very personal things mentioned, things no one else should know. It said he knew those were the best pair I own and that I shave bare down there. It said in big bold letters that 'I know Alex demands that you keep your pussy shaved clean'. Those were his exact words. He went into great detail explaining all about what Alex and I…well, what our sex life is like. He also detailed that he knows Alex likes rough sex some times. Rory, I'm so embarrassed. I hope you don't think any less of me."

She watched as Rory's eyes went from the ice-cold blue to a passionate violet.

Rory did something totally unexpected—she took Nikki in her arms and held her. Running her hands through Nikki's hair, she pushed it back from her face. "Baby, nothing you say could embarrass me. I've seen it all and done it all. I could never think badly of you, no matter what. You are the kindest, gentlest person I've ever met. You'll get through this, they'll find him and we'll laugh about it in a couple of months." She continued to hold and soothe her.

Nikki felt her chuckling before she heard it.

Rory wanted to relieve some of the embarrassment Nikki felt. "By the way lots of us shave completely bare down there. I personally don't find it romantic to have to stop what I'm doing to pick a hair out of my mouth." This brought a roar of laughter from both of them.

Nikki smiled. "Well that's one way to put it. And here I was worried that you might be offended by some of the things."

"I take it you're feeling better now? Why don't you splash some cold water on your face so your eyes don't get too puffy? I'll make you some fresh tea. As far as offending me, that could never happen. Remember I'm one of those girls your mother warned you about. I'm one of the original bad girls." She held out her hand, helping Nikki from the couch.

Still in the bathroom drying her face, Nikki heard the front door being thrown open and Alex shouting. "Oh no. She's going to go off the deep end seeing Rory here." Fear coursed through her. Nikki knew neither of them had done anything wrong, but Alex wouldn't believe it. She feared what Alex would do to Rory. Feeling nauseous, Nikki had to lean on the sink for a moment to get her nerves under control. She couldn't let Alex see her like this.

"Nikki where are you? Nikki?"

Scott was right behind her. He hadn't wanted Alex to go into the house alone, knowing the mood she was in.

Alex slammed the door. "Nikki, where the fuck are you?"

Scott put his hand on her shoulder. "Alex, calm down. I'm sure she's all right. The bathroom door just opened."

Scott continued into the kitchen where he heard a teakettle whistling. Nikki came out of the small downstairs bathroom, saying hello to him as he passed her in the hallway.

"Alex, I'm right here. I was in the bathroom. I'm okay love, just a little shaken." She flew into Alex's arms, letting her hold her tightly.

Alex kissed her neck and whispered in her ear that all was okay, now that she was there. However, in the back of her mind, Alex told herself not to show her anger about Rory being there.

†

The two women were getting close and Alex didn't like it. Nikki was hers and hers alone. For the moment though, she would put up with Rory. Alex followed the motto of 'keep your friends close and your enemies even closer'.

Alex even tried the scare tactic to keep them from getting close. She cornered Rory in the parking lot one day. They had a frank chat. It was then that Rory told her not to worry, she was already involved with someone. Alex asked her why Nikki hadn't mentioned anything about that. Rory guiltily informed her that Nikki didn't know, that she hadn't told her.

Letting Rory know she wasn't too pleased, Alex urged her to reconsider how close they were getting. Rory took it as a threat. However, she was not about to back down. After cornering Rory that day, Alex let Nikki know that night who she truly belonged to.

✝

A few days later, it was still dark out when Nikki left for work. Alex had taken to leaving long before she awoke, so she could go to the gym before the station. In the darkness, Nikki didn't see the figure standing on the back deck, watching as she raced around, trying to find her cell phone and keys.

This particular morning it was even more fun than usual as the 'shadow' held up Nikki's extra set of keys and jingled them in the morning darkness. At Nikki's request, Alex had obtained another set of house and vehicle keys after the last time they had disappeared.

After a half hour of searching, Nikki gave up. She called Alex to find out where she put the spare set. Not being able to find those either, Alex had Scott swing by and take her to work. "I'd come get you myself, but I'm at the courthouse waiting to testify and I can't leave."

"That's okay. Thank you for calling Scott. I can't imagine where they can be."

"Don't worry. We'll find them later. If not we have the whole weekend to get new ones." Alex said.

Arriving late to work did nothing to help her distracted mind. She couldn't imagine what had happened to the items this time. Several times now, things had gone missing and she was starting to get a little spooked. Putting all thought aside, Nikki sat down at her desk and jumped into her work.

Later that night she sat in bed trying to read. After several pages, Nikki realized she didn't have a clue what she'd just read. Closing the book, she set it on the bed. Her mind drifted to the conversation she had with Liz the night before.

Nikki had agreed to meet Liz at her favorite Mexican restaurant. Luckily, the place was almost empty so no one would overhear their conversation. Liz knew that something was going on when she talked to Nikki the week before. She knew briefly about the letters, but never thought they would start to escalate as they had.

Nikki told her a little more of what the letters to Alex contained.

Liz was speechless. "I, uh, wow. That's intense. I want you to keep your cell phone with you at all times, Nikki. If you need to, call me anytime and I'll come running. Oh, I wanted to ask you…" Liz spied the waiter coming toward them. She would wait until he was gone.

Gut instinct told her Alex was capable of many things, but what she heard shocked her. She realized two months after she met Alex that the detective was a volatile woman. She also had suspicions that Alex was responsible for the bruises Nikki sometimes sported. Liz was certain too that Alex had broken her arm.

Liz had tried on numerous occasions to talk to Nikki about it, but she always denied it or changed the subject. Then this new woman came along. Liz immediately liked her. Something told her Rory wouldn't take any shit from Alex. She also had an inkling that Nikki found Rory fascinating.

The waiter walked away after placing their meals on the table. Liz thought she might as well jump in with both feet. "Nikki, how's Rory working out? She seems really intelligent. How does she get along with Alex?"

Nikki contemplated as she chewed. "She's fantastic. I think she's way over qualified. She may even be over-qualified for my position. I don't understand why she would take a job like this. Actually, Alex is remodeling one of the rooms in her house at the moment. She's a really nice person." Nikki's smile gave Liz her answer.

"So you think she's nice huh? What about good looking?"

Nikki hesitated. She wasn't sure how to answer her friend.

"Come on, you have to admit she is one hot looking woman. If I was into women, I'd be trying everything I could to get her into bed. Come on be honest, you wouldn't mind her stoking your fire?" Liz finished off her margarita, motioning for the waiter to bring her another.

Nikki contemplated her friend's words as she pushed the last of her enchilada around the plate. She had to admit there was something about her. Something drew Nikki to her even knowing she couldn't count on Rory's friendship for long. Alex would soon scare Rory away.

The only reason Liz was still around was because Alex didn't see her as a threat. Whereas Rory—well, Alex was probably already subtly telling her to back off, that Nikki belonged to her.

Yet those eyes, she was drawn to them. So could she tell her no? Only if she thought Alex would never find out. "No." She looked up at Liz.

"Yes, she is a good friend. I would never and I repeat never, cheat on Alex. I couldn't. You know that fact as well as I do. I don't want to lose her as a friend though. She's a good person, I enjoy talking to her." Nikki pushed away her plate, unable to finish her food.

"I think maybe you should talk to her about Alex. You need someone to talk to other than me. Maybe she can add new perspective to everything." Polishing off her second drink, Liz threw money on the table for the bill.

"Liz, I can't do that. You know that. I don't want to lose her as a friend. If she knew what Alex is capable of, she'd turn around and run as fast as she could. No, I can't do that. I can't tell her. I don't want her to think less of me." Maybe Millie had been right and she was not ever meant to be happy. Nikki was on the verge of tears. No, there was no way she could confide in Rory. It was bad enough that Liz knew what little that she did.

†

One week later Nikki was just dozing off when she felt Alex sit down on the bed. Alex didn't speak. She just sat there very still. Nikki could tell she was deep in thought. She reached over, putting her hand on Alex's thigh. Feeling Alex tense, it was then that she could feel the anger rolling off her.

Nikki wasn't sure what had triggered Alex's mood. The only thing she could think of was that Alex was pissed off because she'd worked late all week on the project they were behind on. Of course, it could also have been that Rory drove her to and from work for the past two days.

Alex didn't think it safe for Nikki to drive to work alone since the arrival of the box. She would have taken her but she and Scott had spent the past few days following up on some leads. Alex thanked Rory when she suggested she play chauffer. She knew Nikki wouldn't be stupid enough to let her try anything funny.

Nikki had known what the consequences would be if she did. Yet…what Alex had seen that evening made Alex furious at Nikki. She belonged to Alex alone. No one touched her property.

Sitting on the edge of the bed, Alex thought back to what she witnessed hours before. She had gotten home late, well after ten o'clock. The first thing she noticed was Rory's Porsche in the driveway. Quietly she walked into the kitchen. There she found Nikki crying with Rory holding her, caressing her cheek.

Alex wanted nothing more than to kill the woman on the spot for touching Nikki. It took all she could not to pull her gun and blow her head off. Rory gradually pulled away from her and Nikki blew her nose.

Unknown to Alex, Rory had heard her come in. She wasn't about to pull away from Nikki. They'd done nothing wrong. She was doing nothing more than comforting a friend who was terrified that something was going to happen to her spouse.

Rory turned to find Alex's eyes glued to her. It was then she knew for sure how dangerous Alex was. There was no doubt what Alex wanted to do. Rory's eyes showed no recognition that Alex's hand was on her gun.

She met Alex's glare dead on, not about to give into the woman. If she did, it would give Alex the upper hand. Each stood throwing daggers and non-verbal threats at one another.

Nikki was clueless as to what had transpired during those few seconds. After blowing her nose, she washed her hands. When she turned back, Rory was almost to the door, saying good night for the evening and confirming that she would pick her up at seven the next morning.

It was then that Nikki noticed Alex looked upset. Pulling dinner from the oven where she had been keeping it warm, Nikki tried to explain. "Sorry,

I guess it just hit me all at once that there is someone out there stalking us."

Shoveling food into her mouth, Alex looked up. "Never forget who you belong to, my love."

Nikki had a headache and retired right after eating. Alex stayed up, finishing off a bottle of Scotch and several more beers.

Alex turned the nightstand light on when she came to bed.

"Alex love, are you okay? You've been quiet since you got home." Nikki started to sit up pulling the covers up with her. She always slept in the nude, the way Alex liked her to. "Alex…"

Before Nikki knew what had happened, Alex was on top of her. All she could smell was beer and Scotch. She knew Alex had been downing the scotch as if it was water, now she feared the worst. Metal touched her wrists then her arms were pulled above her head. Alex had just handcuffed her to the bed.

"Alex, what are you doing? Please talk to me."

Nikki looked into Alex's eyes. She saw only darkness. Her eyes were almost completely black. She was angry, extremely angry. It was then that Nikki realized she'd never seen Alex this out of control. Fear consumed Nikki, spreading through into her heart.

"You are mine and mine alone. Do you understand that? Do you?" Alex slapped her across the face. "No one touches what is mine. I've put up with it for long enough now. I thought perhaps you had learned your lesson last time." With that, Alex traced the scar that her carving had left on Nikki.

"I'm going to teach you once and for all. You're MINE!" Alex got up from the bed and went to her dresser. Opening the bottom drawer, she pulled out the items she wanted. She'd teach her, no doubt about that. "Close your eyes and do not, I repeat, do not, make a peep."

Nikki's heart beat faster, not knowing what to expect. It was going to be a long night and she knew she'd have bruises in the morning. Then she felt it. Something clamped onto her nipples. She found the pressure to be pleasurable but just as suddenly, that pleasure turned to pain. It hurt. It was not possible…this couldn't be happening.

Alex had put the nipple clamps on gently. She knew Nikki would like them. Then she started to tighten them. Alex wanted to hear her scream. Then she could punish her for that as well.

Mesmerized, she watched as Nikki enjoyed it. She wondered how she'd react to them being tighter. "Oh, yeah, now we're getting somewhere, you're starting to squirm." Alex tightened them some more.

On the final twist, Nikki couldn't stop, she cried out, begging Alex to loosen them. "Please Alex, they hurt. Please loosen them."

"No, I'm going to leave them that tight because you weren't supposed to make a sound and you did, so you must be taught to be a good girl. Now, close those eyes again." She pushed Nikki's legs farther apart.

"Keep your legs apart just like that. I know how you like to spread them wide. Do you spread them for her, too?"

Nikki shook her head no. She knew better than to talk.

Alex pushed her legs as far apart as humanly possible. Laying spread eagled, the outside of her legs rested on the bed. "That's a good little girl…so far apart, such easy access. Only a ho can spread them that far. Are you my ho? Speak!" She pushed down on Nikki's legs, causing the muscles to pull, causing her additional pain.

"Yes, I'm yours, only yours…."

She stroked Nikki's clit, feeling how wet she was. Alex enjoyed knowing she was the cause of it. "Ooh so wet. You must be enjoying those on your tits and don't try to deny it because you're dripping wet. Now what should your punishment be? I know what you'd like."

She picked up one of the toys she'd retrieved from the drawer. Running it through Nikki's wetness, she lubricated it. Roughly, Alex pulled Nikki's clit, hard enough to lift her off the bed.

Nikki felt the pleasure of the stroke when Alex touched her. Then she felt the toy. Even through the pain in her nipples, it excited her. Her heart began to race. Then she felt the pull on her clit when Alex lifted her from the bed.

It hurt slightly when Alex pulled on her. Nikki then felt the toy being buried inside her. It startled her when it was roughly rammed it into her. Usually Alex was gentler at first.

Alex lowered Nikki's body back onto the bed and closed her legs. "Stay just like that. Hold that in you. Don't move until I tell you too."

She crawled off the bed and stood. Slowly putting on the leather harness, she inserted a new dildo she'd bought, just for such an occasion. It was larger than any she had previously owned. She couldn't wait to use it on Nikki. Picking up the bottle of lubricant, she applied a generous amount. Crawling back onto the bed, Alex moved in front of Nikki as she pulled her legs apart.

"Are you ready for your surprise? Just keep your eyes closed." Laying Nikki's legs open wide, she pulled the smaller one out. Parting Nikki, she touched the tip of it to her opening.

"Ready? Just nod yes."

Nikki nodded, even though she was afraid. Her mind had not prepared her for what she felt. The stench of the alcohol once more wafted down from above her. It seemed to ooze out every pore of Alex's body.

Alex forcefully rammed into her. It was too large in every way, but Alex continued.

Tears came to Nikki's eyes. She was in pain, greater pain than anything before.

Pulling out, Alex grunted as she slammed back into her. "You like that? Are you dreaming that it's her fucking you? Well, it's not and it never will be. It's me. It will always be me."

The assault continued. Nikki couldn't take much more. Alex pulled the dildo almost out. She looked down at Nikki. "Mine. You belong to me."

She then slammed into her a final time. It was all Nikki could take, she screamed. Nikki pulled against the handcuffs that held her in place.

Nikki sobbed. "Please Alex, please, you're hurting me, please stop. I'm begging you, please stop."

Alex was no longer in control and Nikki knew it. This person above her was no longer her lover. The animal within her had taken over. It was that which attacked her, not her lover, not Alex.

Nikki knew she had to do something. Faking an orgasm was the only option left open to her. Thinking Nikki was coming set off Alex. She laid down on top of Nikki, leaving the dildo in her. Her mouth rested on Nikki's left ear.

"If she or anyone ever touches you again, I'll kill them. That is after I torture them. Do you understand? Do not ever consider leaving me. If you do, I will hunt you down and kill whoever you are with and then I'll kill you, after I do unspeakable things to you, do you understand? Speak, tell me you understand." To push her point home, she pulled the dildo out and thrust it back in as hard as she could.

Nikki was weak and in so much pain, she was ready to pass out. She had begged her to stop. She had pleaded with her. Then the vow.... She knew Alex meant it. Nikki knew without a doubt, Alex would do the things she said. Her heart cried. There would be no help for her, she couldn't allow it. She couldn't allow anyone to be hurt because of her.

"Yes, I understand. I am yours and yours alone."

†

After looking at herself in the mirror the next morning, Nikki really didn't want to venture out into the world. She looked like something a cat would hack up onto the floor and felt even worse.

The booze that Alex consumed had taken its toll on her as well. Alex remained where she had passed out hours earlier, lying on the floor where she had fallen after trying to stand. Nikki tried to get her onto the bed, but she was too big and too heavy.

Nikki slowly took a shower, letting the steaming water work on the sore muscles. She washed the tender areas carefully. She had to use a panty liner because she was still bleeding slightly. Nikki then put on the most comfortable clothing she had, a pair of sweatpants and a sweatshirt.

She needed something mindless to do as she tried to process what had occurred. Finally, Nikki decided to do the weekly grocery shopping, it was very early and the store would be almost empty. Shopping was something she could do in her sleep because she bought almost the same items every week. Nikki texted Rory to tell her not to worry about picking her up, that they could complete the project on Monday.

Hoping Alex would be awake and have sobered up by the time she got back, she quietly left. When she got back, Nikki knew what would happen. Alex would apologize then promise never to do it again.

By the time she left the house, Nikki had convinced herself that this would be the time Alex would change. *We've hit rock bottom, the only way now is up*, she thought.

Alex's outbursts had been getting worse and more frequent. No longer was she able to control her anger.

In Alex's tormented mind, this was acceptable behavior and Nikki did nothing to dissuade her. She never fought back. *I know I'm enabling her to continue, that was what Kirstin had said. She's right, but what can I do about it? Nothing...I can do nothing.*

Rounding the corner of the cereal aisle Nikki ran into one of those people she wished never to see again—her ex, Ann. She stood transfixed, not able to say a word. The other woman was equally stunned. It had a long time since they had run into one another.

"Ann, it's been a long time. How have you been?" Nikki tried to push down the anger rising in her. Just seeing this woman pushed all the wrong buttons. She hated her with a passion.

"I'm doing okay. Better than you by the looks of it. Nikki, what happened? Did Alex do this?" She touched her hand to Nikki's face. "I would have never hurt you like this. I'm sorry. I guess it's none of my business. Other than, I still love you. Are you sure you're happy with her? I miss you terribly and am so lonely without you. I'd do anything to get you back."

Nikki was disgusted. She couldn't believe Ann could even contemplate asking her to come back to her. Nikki was even more disgusted with herself.

She should have put something on to cover up the bruise. However, she didn't think she would run into anyone she knew this early in the morning. Her luck had deserted her today. Things could only get worse.

"Ann, not even if you were the last woman on earth. You've already caused me enough heartache. Why would I invite more? I love Alex, we are very happy, and no, she didn't cause the bruise on my face. How dare you assume that! Now if you'll excuse me I have things to do and they do not include you." Nikki started to walk away.

"Nikki, just remember my offer. If things get too bad with her, please come to me."

Grabbing the rest of the items she needed, Nikki got out of the store as fast as she could. Seeing Ann again had unsettled her, especially after the previous night.

Nikki found Alex in the kitchen drinking a cup of coffee when she arrived home. Alex moved to her like a panther pouncing on its prey. Caressing Nikki's face she tried to find the words she wanted to say. This was the hardest thing she ever had to do. Before the past couple of years, she'd never apologized to anyone for anything. It seemed all she did these days was apologize. Most of the time Nikki was the one on the receiving end of things.

Alex took the bags from her, setting them on the counter. "Honey, I'll get the rest of them. Sit down, have a cup of coffee, and relax." She poured a fresh cup, handed it to her, and headed out the door.

Twenty minutes later, everything was in from the car and put away. Nikki sat the whole time wondering when the other shoe would drop. Alex stood next to her and ran her fingers through Nikki's hair. She leaned over, touched her lips to her cheek, and whispered 'I love you'. Nikki turned to face her.

"Alex…" Her words were swallowed when Alex kissed her. The kiss lingered and Nikki felt her anger thawing.

"Baby, I can't begin to tell you how sorry I am. I don't know what is happening with me lately. I can't seem to control my anger. I just feel like I'm losing control over what's going on with all this shit. I want to catch the bastard that is doing this and then get on with our lives. I am just so sorry."

Nikki took Alex's hands in hers and squeezed. She contemplated carefully what she was going to say. At least Alex was now admitting she was out of control.

"Alex, I love you very much, you know that right?"

Alex nodded.

"I agree with you though. You get so angry lately. Then you drink too much and let the anger take control. My love, we'll get through this. I know you'll find whoever is doing this. Just, please don't do anything…that will make it so I lose you. I don't want you to get into any trouble. You can't go on like this anymore. Please do this for me. For us.…"

Alex felt the tears and she did nothing to stop them. Gathering Nikki in her arms, she held her. Together the two of them shed the tears that have been building for several weeks.

Finally collecting her nerve, Alex asked an even harder question. "Baby, I um, I didn't hurt you last night, did I? I don't remember much. Did I give you this bruise?" She touched Nikki's face. Her heart hurt when she thought about the bruise.

"Do you want me to make you something to eat? You must be hungry, would you like something to eat?" Nikki went to move away when Alex caught her arm.

"Nikki, are you hurt? Do you need to go to the doctor?" Alex's eyes pleaded with her.

Nikki saw the fear in them. She had never seen fear from Alex before. It scared her and shook her.

"Love, it's nothing that won't heal. Okay? Now, what do you want to eat?" She opened the refrigerator. "I bought that ham from the deli that you like, would you like a sandwich or I could make you an omelet. Which would you prefer?"

"Nik, I would like for you to please stand still for a second so I can make sure you're okay. Besides the bruise on your face, what else? Did I hurt you anywhere else? Please, I need to know." She held Nikki, terrified at the answer. "Please tell me what I did."

Nikki sat down on the stool at the island. She motioned for Alex to sit beside her. She then told Alex all that had happened the night before.

Alex was mortified at what she had done. She couldn't even look Nikki in the eyes. She lowered her head to rest in her hands, her elbows on the island. "Oh God, what have I done. I... I...How can I ever ask you to forgive me for that? I can't, there is no forgiveness for that. FUCK!"

Pounding her fists on the counter, Alex knew their lives couldn't go on like this. She could not continue to hurt Nikki. She loved her more than life itself. This time she knew she'd gone too far. She hadn't stopped when Nikki begged her to. There was no way around it. She'd done the unthinkable.

Grabbing Nikki's wrists, Alex pushed back the sleeves. There she found the marks from the handcuffs. Looking into Nikki's eyes, she felt ashamed. Never before had she felt such shame. There was no way around the truth this time. She had handcuffed Nikki to the bed and raped her. The admission rocked her to her core.

"I need to…I need to go take care of something. I'll be back later." Alex had her hand on the doorknob. She stopped but didn't look back. "I love you, baby, more than anything, always remember that Nikki." She walked out the door into the darkening skies.

†

Nikki needed to change the sheets. She stood by the bed, looking down at the top sheet that lay crumpled on the floor. She tensed when her eyes landed upon the soiled bottom sheet. The air smelled ripe, a stale smell, a smell you would associate with an orgy having occurred there.

Yes, an orgy of sorts had gone on, all of it one sided. She gaped at the bottom sheet in stunned silence. The reality of the pain between her thighs once more hit home. Staring at the patches of blood, Nikki trembled with fear. Fear of the unknown.

No, that was not quite right. She knew who she feared. When had the love she held turned to fear?

"No, I love her... I don't fear her. You're not supposed to fear the one you love," she said aloud.

She pulled the sheets from the bed, took them to the first floor, and stuffed them in the washer.

Nikki didn't know what to do with herself. She was antsy. Deciding to do what she always did when she was upset, Nikki went shopping. Yes, the mall that was the ticket. She did some of her best thinking in the mall. All she knew was that she had to get out of the house.

As she started the vehicle, a worse fear startled her. What if Alex never came back? Could she live without her? The answer to that was a double-edged sword. No, she could not live without her, nor could she continue as they had been.

Tears streamed and hearts ached.

†

At the mall, Nikki bought a pretzel and soda. She always thought better when munching on something. Finding a seat, Nikki relaxed to enjoy her treat. Almost done, she heard her name called.

Hearing Rory gasp, she casually lifted her eyes. Anger was clearly written on Rory's face. Nikki had been beaten both physically and mentally off and on through her whole life. Two people had now raped her. Someone she loathed and someone she loved more than life itself. How was one different from the other?

Now that she had arrived at a point when she could take no more, Nikki was confronted with the unspoken fury of yet another person in her life.

Before Nikki stood a woman that she had come to trust. A woman whose opinion she valued. Was Rory upset with her for staying with Alex and allowing it to continue? Or was her anger directed at Alex herself?

Nikki bowed her head, finding she couldn't withstand the scrutiny of the other woman. She started to say hello but all that came forth was a squeak. Mortified, Nikki retreated further from everything around her.

Rory brought her hand forward slowly. Cupping the left side of Nikki's face, she softly caressed down her chin. Gently lifting Nikki's face toward her, she choked when she looked upon the battered face once more.

"Oh, Nikki…"

Chapter Three

Reckonings and Consequences

Alex ran to the only place that could be of comfort at this point in her life. She couldn't go to Scott's house. She couldn't let Tessa find out what she had done. Alex already had the feeling Scott's wife was pissed off at her about something so she wasn't about to give her further ammunition.

What had she done to the woman she loved more than life? Alex fully expected Nikki never to forgive her for this. Not this time. Alex deserved to rot in hell for what she'd done.

Pulling into Kirstin's driveway, it hit her. "I'm no better than Nikki's stepfather who beat her just for fun or the bastard who had raped her. I'm supposed to protect her against shit like this, not be the cause of it."

Alex felt ignorant and stupid. She'd reopened old wounds, reawakening feelings of fear and helplessness in the woman she would die for.

Alex pounded her head on the steering wheel. "She'll never forgive me for this, never! Oh God, what have I done?"

She gazed out the truck window at her sister's house, knowing this was her last refuge in life. What if Kirstin turned her away? No, her sister would not.

Alex loved her sister dearly. She admired Kirstin for being the voice of reason, while she could only dig herself deeper without even opening her mouth.

Walking up to the house, Alex did something she hadn't in years. She rang the doorbell. She felt undeserving just to walk in as if she belonged there, as if she was family. She felt she deserved to be left standing out in the cold.

Kirstin looked through the window in the door. "What the hell?" she mouthed. Immediately she knew something was wrong. Alex never rang the bell. Kirstin threw the door open, looking at Alex closely. "You look like hell. Get in here."

Pulling Alex into the hallway, she slammed the door behind them. Kirstin took her sister by the arm. Noticing Alex was upset, she led her into the living room, to the sofa. Crossing the room, Kirstin poured her a drink.

Alex sat looking at the drink in Kirstin's hand. She looked at the glass as if it was about to sprout wings and fly off.

"No… No thanks." Holding up her hand, she stopped Kirstin from coming any closer with the drink. "I think it might be a while before I have another one."

Downing the drink herself, Kirstin knew this was going to be a rough conversation. What had her sister done this time? Sitting next to Alex, she waited. They sat for several long moments, the silence lingering like a death in the room.

Alex looked at Kirstin then back down at the floor. Shuffling her feet, she tried buying herself a little more time, not knowing where to start.

Kirstin cleared her throat. It had to be bad, really bad for Alex to look so distraught.

Alex looked up at her. Seeing the sympathy, she broke. "Oh God, Kir, I fucked up so bad this time, I don't see any way to ever make it right." Alex started rocking backing forth on the sofa, just as she did when she was a child.

Kirstin grasped Alex's shaking hands. "I love you, sis, no matter what. Tell me."

The contact opened the dam and the river flowed. "She'll never forgive me, never. How could I expect her to? She needs to leave me, to get as far away from me as she can. I can't help myself anymore. I can't seem to stop it. I can't stop the anger and darkness from taking over."

She couldn't stop the tears. She didn't want to stop them. If her tears were made of acid, burning her face, Alex knew she would deserve it. She deserved much worse. She should be in jail for what she had done.

Kirstin gathered her into her arms and rocked her. It was the same as in their childhood…The younger even-tempered sibling comforting the older wild-child sister.

"Alex sweetie, I'm always here for you. I'm your friend as well as your sister. You need to talk to me, tell me what happened. There is always a way to find forgiveness, but you have to confront the problem first. I know there have been problems for some time now and I knew this day would come eventually. Talk to me please."

Alex let her sister hold her as she told her what happened. She started from when she'd been shot. Alex knew that was when life had really started to spiral out of control. Kirstin sat listening.

Suddenly Alex stopped talking.

Kirstin felt her sister's body stiffen. Alex was getting to the incident that sent her running to her safe haven. Something told Kirstin they were now at the heart of the issue. "Alex, what happened last night after you got home?"

Alex started to shake violently. Never before had Kirstin been so terrified for her sister. Trying not to let that terror show in her voice, she urged Alex to go on.

"Alex, what happened? I won't judge you. You're doing enough of that to yourself. You have to forgive yourself first. Please, Alex, talk to me, were you drunk?"

Alex's tears now turned to sobs.

"Nothing will excuse what I did. I had a few beers and polished off a bottle of Scotch. I was so angry finding Rory there, touching…holding her. I just drank and drank. Then later when I went upstairs…I saw her lying on the bed, it went through my mind again. My mind went from seeing them together in the kitchen to being in bed together. Kir, I couldn't stop, I was so angry. She begged me to stop and I didn't. The more she begged the angrier I got. I don't remember all that happened. Oh God, Kirstin what am I going to do? How can I ever ask her for forgiveness this time? How can I ever be near her again? Without feeling…I'm so ashamed. Kirstin, I don't know what to do. I'll do anything to make it up to her."

Kirstin pushed Alex's wet hair from her face. "Sweetie, the first thing you need to do is stop drinking. The second is to rid yourself of the jealousy. Nikki loves you and you alone. She's not the type of person to cheat on you. She's loyal to a fault, and truthfully, I don't know why she's stuck with you this long. You need to put the anger into other things. Start to build furniture again. You loved to do that. The two of you should go to a couple's counselor. I love her as much as you. Don't get me wrong, but she's an enabler. Nikki should've kicked your ass out, instead of making excuses."

Alex knew she was right, but could she tell another living soul what she had done? No, she couldn't. Telling your sister was one thing, but a complete stranger? No, she could not.

"This is private, Kirstin. I couldn't talk about this to a complete stranger. Nikki and I need to be able to work this out ourselves. If I went to see someone and the department found out, I'd lose my job. I can't risk that." She shook her head.

"Not even if that is what it will take to save this relationship? Is your job worth that much? God damn it, Alex, sometimes you are so selfish." Kirstin stood, pacing the room as she lit into Alex.

Alex thought to herself a moment, the truth dawning on her. Was her job truly more important? It made her who she was. Without being a cop, she was nothing. It is what she was born to be. Nothing would stop her from being who she was. No, nothing was more important than being a cop. Without it, she was nothing.

"Are you willing to risk her love just to keep your job? I would think she'd mean more than anything in the world to you. I don't want to see the two of you split up, but maybe you need to be apart for a little time to get yourself together. Do you understand what I'm trying to say?" Kneeling in front of her, she held Alex's hands in hers.

Alex laid her head on their hands.

"Alex, you need to get your life together before you can ever expect Nikki to forgive you. We have the extra room downstairs that you can have if you want. I know someone that you can go see and the department won't know anything about it. Alex, I know that look on your face. You can't continue on like this. Do you think you'll be able to turn it all around on your own?"

The look in her eyes told Kirstin everything she needed to know. She wouldn't go for help. She would try to work it out on her own with no professional help. In the end, nothing would truly change.

"Kirstin, I don't want anyone else to know about this. I don't even want Tom to know about it. What can't you understand about that?" Alex stood, starting for the door. "I should've known it was a mistake coming here."

Kirstin attached herself to Alex as she walked by her. "Alex, please don't do this. I'll beg, if I have to. Don't think you can continue to take on the world by yourself. You need help."

Alex stopped in her tracks. "I thought that's why I was here. I came to talk to you, to ask you for help and all you tell me is I need to blabber about it to a stranger. That's not going to happen, not in this lifetime. So don't fucking push it, Kirstin. I came to *you* for help...." Alex pulled her arm from Kirstin's grip and walked out the door.

Kirstin rested her head on the doorframe. "Oh God, this is not going to end well. Not well at all. Shit, what am I going to do?"

She let the tears flow freely.

✝

It took Nikki a moment to find her voice. It seemed to have taken a vacation temporarily. "Hello Rory. It's not what you are thinking."

Rory sat next to her.

Rory tried to calm her rage, not wanting to say something she shouldn't. She especially didn't want to cause a scene in the mall. Closing her eyes, she pulled her inner strength to the surface. She hoped Nikki would open up to her, not continue the charade.

Taking a deep breath, Rory jumped in with both feet. "Nikki, you probably don't want to know what I'm thinking at this moment. Besides, I don't think they draw and quarter people any longer. Or put their bodies on pikes on the front lawn of the castle either. Do you want to talk about it or are we going to just ignore it like all the other times?"

Nikki looked at her then turned away. She watched the people scurrying in and out of the stores, looking for one of those last minute bargains.

Rory expected Nikki would withdraw. She wasn't quite sure why she continued to push the envelope. It puzzled her why keeping this woman from being hurt further meant so much to her.

It occurred to Rory that she could take Nikki away from all that was going on. Shocked, Rory wondered where that thought had come from. Rory blamed it on that she just really needed to get laid. If only Lydia would arrive soon.

Of course, they did have an open relationship.

Rory knew that would never happen. Nikki would stay with Alex, no matter what. What she didn't understand was why. Why wouldn't Nikki leave Alex? Maybe if Nikki had confidence in herself. Maybe if she realized she could do better.

Nikki looked back at Rory. She saw something in her eyes, something different. She'd only ever seen that look in Alex's eyes. Maybe she'd been mistaken, because the look only lasted a second before confusion replaced it.

Rory broke the spell. "Are you okay?" She laid her hand on Nikki's thigh and squeezed gently. She never expected Nikki's reaction.

Nikki jumped as if startled, flinching in pain. This confirmed Rory's suspicions. She knew there were bruises, other than just on her face. She knew that pattern of abuse. She had seen it before, having lived through it personally.

"Nikki, let's go to the restaurant over here. We'll sit at the bar and have a drink. Okay? Come on." Pulling Nikki up, Rory pushed her toward the door.

"Rory, I shouldn't. Alex might be home soon. I really should get going." She stepped back as if she were going to leave.

Rory put a hand on her arm. "Please don't. Have a drink with me and we'll chat for a little while. I think you need it."

Walking through the door, Rory informed the hostess they were going to sit at the bar. She ordered a drink for each of them. Waiting for the bartender to leave, she studied the area around them. Maybe if she started talking about something else, Rory could get out of Nikki what was going on.

Rory had to try at least. "Nikki, I'd like to think we've become friends. I also like to think you could come to me with anything. I would never judge anyone, you know that. What's going on? I heard it mentioned that you lost your sister six months ago and Alex's parents not that long ago. That kind of stress is enough to make any person a little edgy. Maybe talking about it will help. Were you close with your sister?"

Rory didn't expect the reaction she received.

Nikki laughed so hard it brought tears to her eyes. "Uh no, we weren't close. We hadn't actually spoken in a very long time. She thought I was the spawn of Satan himself. So you can understand when the hospital called to tell me that she had a severe allergic reaction to some medication and had died, well, I couldn't really feel much sorrow."

Nikki spent the next hour telling Rory all about her sister, Millie. Then she confessed the mother of all confessions.

"I really feel no remorse that she is dead. Is that so wrong? Does that make me evil? When I went to clean out her house, I was tempted to call someone to just go and take it all away without my ever really looking at it. I only ever wanted her love and understanding, not her material possessions. I didn't really think I was asking for the world but maybe I was."

Rory motioned for another round. They were going to be there for a while, so she ordered several appetizers as well. She still held out hope that Nikki would unburden herself with what had happened the previous evening.

Rory, during their conversation, had finally told Nikki she had a girlfriend. Nikki wasn't sure how she felt about the revelation. She was relieved, yet hurt at the same time. Mentally Nikki pulled slightly away, hoping to regain her thoughts.

Picking up her drink, Nikki studied it for a moment before taking a sip. Then she took a longer drink.

"Hell, while I'm on a roll I might as well keep going, huh." She looked at Rory expecting to see horror in her eyes. What she found was the strength to continue.

"Only if you want, if it's too much, we can stop." Rory didn't want to push too hard. Nikki needed to unburden herself —that was apparent to Rory.

"Thanks. We used to call him Pap-Pap. He must have been in his seventies. Everyone in the neighborhood loved him and his wife. They seemed like your typical grandparents. What they never knew was that he was sick, very sick. Mom used to ask them to watch me once in a while when she had to go out and couldn't take me. When mom got sick and had the miscarriages, they left me with them for several days. But his behavior had started even before that.

"I never said anything to anyone. I always thought everything was my fault, that I deserved it all. He… used to touch me where he shouldn't have touched any child. The worst was when…God." A shiver ran down her body.

"Nikki, let's stop. You don't need to talk any more about this." She held Nikki's hand tighter.

"Yes, I do. I have to get this out now, while I have the courage. Maybe talking about it will help me deal with it and put it behind me. I tried to talk to Alex about it once, but…I don't know. It made me think she would see me as spoiled goods. I know that sounds stupid, but I'm ashamed it happened."

She squeezed Rory's hand to convey her thanks.

"Nikki, I'm your friend. I will help you in any way I can. We've become close during the past couple of months. You know in your heart that you can trust me. Sometimes it is easier to confide in someone that is not a spouse." Rory more than wanted her to confide in her. She needed Nikki to trust her, to have faith she'd protect her.

"I know what you mean. The old saying that your family is what you make it. I really feel we have become good friends and I thank you for that. More than I can tell you. So, on I go, I guess. He took me to see the movie *Tommy*. Can you believe that? I have no clue how he got me in to see it. I don't remember if the standards weren't as strict back then or what. Can you believe of all the movies to take a child to…I remember being scared shitless by the images on the screen. During the movie he kept touching me. I've never forgotten that feeling. I just wanted to go home, hide under my bed, and never come out. I knew I couldn't say anything to either of my parents. Mom was so sick and my step-dad of course would've never believed me. Then we moved across town when I was twelve. I found out all about girls that year from Jackie, the girl next door. Wow, she was good." Nikki smiled.

"Jackie taught me all about sex. There was no going back then. Her parents were cool. They loved me and kind of adopted me after they realized what dad was like. Mom just got sicker and spent most of the time in the hospital. Then she died…."

Nikki couldn't stop. She shared all of it with Rory—the good times, the not so good times and the horrific times. However, she held back anything to do with Alex. She didn't want Rory in any danger. Nikki knew she would go after Alex if she knew the whole truth.

Sometime later Rory walked Nikki to her vehicle. Holding the car door open, she grasped Nikki's forearm, stopping her from getting in. Rory pulled her close enough that their bodies almost touched. "If you need me, please call me. Time doesn't matter, only that you call me," she whispered in Nikki's ear.

Nikki shivered when she felt Rory's breath in her ear. She couldn't believe Rory cared so much. What did it mean? She wasn't sure of anything, especially the emotions running through her at that moment.

"Won't my calling in the middle of the night upset your girlfriend? I'm sure she wouldn't take too kindly to being awakened at three in the morning just because I couldn't sleep."

Rory's mind was spinning. She pulled Nikki closer. Words left her lips, finding their way to Nikki's ear, before she could stop them. "Nikki, I'm going to go way out on a limb here. I'm speaking from the heart. You can do better than Alex. She's not good enough for you and she sure as fucking hell doesn't treat you very well. I know you'll always deny it but I know she abuses you. Please know I'll be there for you, no matter what."

Before Nikki knew what was happening Rory took her in her arms and kissed her.

Rory realized what she'd done when she saw the stunned reaction on Nikki's face. She'd done it without conscious thought yet without regret. Rory knew she would kiss her again in a heartbeat and that the words had truly come from her heart. Rational thought seemed to fly away the moment she'd taken Nikki in her arms. They stood with no space between them. A moment of confusion struck Rory. When did they move so close to one another? Nikki's lips were so soft. So hot. Rory wanted to kiss her again. She needed to kiss her again. Rory couldn't though, never again. Rory could see terror in Nikki's eyes.

What had Nikki done to her? When it came to this woman, Rory found she had little control. What she still couldn't understand was why Nikki didn't just leave Alex. To Rory she oozed strength, love, and compassion. Any woman would be lucky to have her, to feel her love. This told Rory that Alex had a hold on her. It was just a matter of finding it and eliminating whatever it was.

Nikki's forehead rested on Rory's chest. "Why?"

Rory pulled Nikki's head up so she could look into her eyes. She saw tears and sadness, where she hoped to see a smiling face. "Why, what?"

She hoped Rory hadn't heard her. How could she explain that her heart had shriveled a long time ago? Nikki hadn't known that she was capable of the emotions she felt any longer. Rory had awakened the buried feelings. If she lied to her, Nikki knew the taller woman would know in a heartbeat. Not able to truly speak from the heart, Nikki came as close as she dared. "You've treated me so wonderfully. So, I guess I was just asking myself why, as in why you and why now? Thank you for everything. I know that sounds corny…thanking you. I think we knew one another in a previous life. That's probably why we feel so close now."

Rory had no idea why she said what she said next. She only wished she could've taken back the words once they were spoken. They cheapened the kiss and all the words after. "Lydia and I have an open relationship."

Nikki's mouth dropped open slightly. She couldn't think. What did Rory's words mean? Why did Rory kiss her? Nikki's mind pondered further. Why did she kiss Rory back or better yet, why did she tell her those things?

"Oh, really…uh…Wow, um. I don't know if I could have that kind of relationship. I kind of like being the only one in Alex's life. I guess I'm a little old fashioned and still believe in monogamy. Still though, if it works for the two of you, I'm happy for you." Nikki knew she was rambling. She was too flustered to try and make sense.

Rory caressed Nikki's face. "Maybe I just never found the right woman to settle down with."

Swiftly she pulled her hand away when she realized what she was doing and saying. She was crossing a line that could only lead to further hurt. She didn't want to lose Nikki as a friend.

Flirting was one thing, but there was a line that once crossed Rory knew she'd lose her. Above all else, Rory knew that Nikki would never cheat on Alex and that she'd protect Alex until death.

Taking a deep breath, Rory stepped back, resigning herself to what she knew to be true. She could never have this woman. Even though in Rory's heart she loved her and would do anything for her - that included letting her go. "I should let you get going. It's late and Alex is probably wondering where you are. Are we still on for the wineries on Saturday?"

Nikki could only nod. With her heart beating out of her chest, Nikki didn't know what to say or think at this point, knowing if she tried, it would come out sounding completely asinine. Instead she chose just to nod and climb into her car. She started the engine as Rory shut the door for her. Rory waved to her as she drove off.

✝

Once back to her truck, Rory got in and sat lost in thought. "I am getting too close to her. I can't, she would hate me for trying to come between her and Alex. I could never live with that. Never. Damn, I wish Lydia was here already." She could feel the wetness pooling between her thighs. Rory shifted in her seat, trying to find a more comfortable position. "I need to go home and take care of this."

✝

Nikki drove home in a daze. With all the emotions buzzing through her, she was petrified of what she felt. She knew it for what it was—lust. "That's all it is. It's because she's been so kind to me."

106

Somewhere, somehow she had found herself starting to really like Rory.

"That can't be," she told herself. "I love Alex. Maybe if we'd met years ago. Not now, it's too late. Oh God, Alex can never know. I would never forgive myself if Alex hurt her — and if Alex knew she kissed me, she'd kill her."

†

Several glorious weeks passed. Alex doted on Nikki every day, and every night she worshiped her body and soul. Every night the detective walked through their front door with a fresh bouquet of roses and a gift. Alex brought her gifts ranging from sapphire pendants that she had custom made, to leather purses from Nikki's favorite store.

Nikki wanted so badly to believe her old Alex was back, she put out of her mind the not so good times they'd had, only focusing on the good. Alex idolized her and that was all that mattered.

Nikki let her guard down, convincing herself all was well with the world.

†

Alex was enraged. Nikki wasn't there when she had arrived home. She'd told Alex she would be home around noon. It was now after two. She looked at her watch once more.

"Where the hell can she be? I refuse to call her on her cell phone. I shouldn't have to track her down. She should just be here where she belongs. She promised me she'd be home…" As an afterthought she added, "Home, where she's safe."

After several hours, the anger turned to fear that Nikki had left her. Alex called Scott. "She's always home when I ask her to be."

Scott told her to chill out. "You know when she's at the mall she loses all track of time. Just call her and be done with it. She won't think you're spying on her, only that you're concerned."

It was as if she hadn't heard a word Scott said. "If she was going to be this late, she should've called me. You don't think that freak has gotten aggressive do you? I was hoping that he would've given up by now and gone away. But no…instead he continues to send the little goodies."

"Alex, you can't think like that every time she leaves the house or every time she's a minute late getting home. If you do, it'll drive you mad. Just relax, okay. Please call her, she'll understand. I'm sure of it." Scott tried his best to calm her fears.

Another thought crossed her mind, a much darker thought. What if Rory had succeeded finally in stealing Nikki from her? The beast within Alex clawed at the surface, roaring to be set free. She would kill. That she knew to be a fact.

"Fine… I'll wait a bit longer, before I go looking for her. Talk to you in the morning. Bye."

A few moments later, Nikki walked through the door, not knowing something was wrong.

Upon seeing Nikki safe and unharmed, her fury returned in full. "Where the fuck have you been?

You said you'd be back by noon, it's now after six, and I'm starving."

✝

Nikki had seen Alex upset many times before. Her lover was trying to rein in her temper. When she saw the vein pulsing on the side of Alex's neck, Nikki knew she was about to explode.

"Alex I'm sorry. Rory called and invited me to lunch. I left you a message on your cell phone. I'm sorry, honey, we kind of talked the afternoon away. I brought Chinese take-out home. I hope that's okay with you."

She looked Alex in the eyes and knew. By the Gods, Alex knew she'd just lied about Rory calling her for lunch. Why did she say that Rory had called her? There was no way she could know that she had run into Rory coming out of the shoe store and proceeded to invite her assistant to lunch. No. There was no way Alex could know that.

Nikki was still unsure why she had done it. The only logical explanation she could come up with was that they hadn't spent any time together during the past several weeks and she was lonely for one of their talks. While having drinks, they talked about almost everything currently going on in each of their lives, yet Alex's name was never once mentioned. Nikki only referred to Alex as she or her.

✝

Alex was still fuming, yet she said nothing. She didn't accuse Nikki of the lie. "Fine.... Let's eat."

Alex sat at the table and waited to be served. The anger in her told her to bide her time, Nikki would soon pay for not obeying her.

✝

Nikki wondered why Alex hadn't accused her of lying. Nikki instead deluded herself and wrapped her mind around warm thoughts that Alex had changed, that she was indeed the old Alex.

They ate in silence. Nikki tried several times to ask Alex about her day. There was something Alex wasn't telling her but she figured she would in time. After Nikki finished loading the dishwasher Alex came into the kitchen. She thought she would try to ask her again.

"Alex honey, did you have a good day. Any interesting new cases?" Nikki saw something in Alex's eyes but she couldn't quite put her finger on it. It was almost as if she was trying to think up something good. Nikki felt like she was covering something up. "Did something happen today, Alex?"

Alex moved so that their bodies were touching. Looking up at her, Nikki saw fire in her eyes.

No, not again. Everything had been going so well.

✝

Anger coursed through Alex. "Yes, I came home and you weren't here. When you weren't home

110

after a while, I thought maybe something happened to you. I told you I like you here when I get home every night, it's where you belong. Home where you're safe, cooking my dinner. Is that so much to ask?" She gripped Nikki's forearm tightly.

"Alex you're hurting my arm. Can you loosen your hand a little, please? I said I was sorry, honey. I'd like to make it up to you."

Nikki knew of only one way to calm her down when she got like this.

Alex knew what Nikki had in mind. "Exactly what I was thinking, baby." Pulling her upstairs to the bedroom, Alex pushed her down on the bed and all but ripped Nikki's clothes from her body. "Why don't you move on up the bed, roll over, and close your eyes?"

Nikki did as she was told to do, the excitement building. She could hear Alex opening a dresser drawer. "Alex, what are you up to?" Her heart rate accelerated, the room turning warmer.

"You'll see, but only if you don't peek and no talking." The bed dipped as Alex climbed on.

"But Alex—"

Alex cut her off before she could finish. She would teach her once and for all whom she belonged to. She would make Nikki want her and her alone. She would take her lover to heights only she could. She would make her beg for more, to relish in what she made her feel.

"Ah, ah, I said no talking. Keep your eyes closed and I'll do the talking. The only time I want to hear you talk is to answer me, okay?" Reaching for her Alex pulled her up on all fours, causing Nikki's wetness to run down her leg.

Nikki liked the way Alex was taking control and being so…what was the word she was looking for?

Alex wanted to know what Nikki was thinking at that moment. "What are you thinking, babe? Tell me. Tell me in words."

Nikki's excitement rocketed. "Powerful…Yes, powerful. In charge. Dominating. Forceful. Wonderful." Nikki loved it when Alex got all butchy. Her excitement grew by the second. Nikki felt Alex reach between her thighs, putting her fingers on the bundle of nerves. She felt it twitch.

Alex pinched Nikki's clit between her fingers. "Do you like that?"

"Yes, so nice." She wiggled her butt to let Alex know how much. She was rewarded for the right answer.

Alex pulled on her clit while pinching it. She pinched a little harder. "How about this, you like this?"

"Oh, yes, do it more, please…" Nikki was gripping the sheets tighter.

Alex rapidly entered her with three fingers, causing Nikki to gasp. "Do you want more?"

"Yes, more please."

Alex pulled out then slid all but her thumb into Nikki, while opening the bottle of lube with the other hand. She poured a generous amount onto the dildo she was wearing. Pulling her hand out of Nikki, she poured some into the palm of her other hand. Alex applied it to the larger one that lay on the bed.

"Are you ready for your surprise? Do you want it?"

"Yes, oh yes, please," Nikki begged.

Alex drizzled extra lube on her rear opening. Nikki knew immediately what she was going to do. She was terrified, yet excited tremendously. Feeling the dildo touch her, she became even more excited. "Are you ready? Tell me you want it."

"Yes, Alex, please." She wiggled her ass again.

Alex squeezed her cheeks hard. "Please what, baby? Tell me or I won't do it."

Nikki found it hard to say. She didn't want it to sound sluttish or worse...corny. She wanted to please Alex. "Alex, please do it."

Alex squeezed them again. "Ah, ah, tell me what you want." She could feel Nikki getting flustered. Alex loved that feeling. She knew she was in control.

"Oh God Alex, fuck me, please. Do to me what I do to you."

"That's better, babe. I like when you tell me what you want. I'm going to go really slow to get you used to it. While I'm taking you back here, I want you to use this on yourself." Alex put a dildo into her hand. It was one of the largest ones Nikki had ever felt. She reached between her thighs as Alex slowly took her from behind.

"Oh, God.... That feels so good. This one's too big though."

"It's not too big, baby. I can fit my hand in you. Now, do it or I stop. Do you understand? When I tell you to do something, you do it. Now do it." Alex growled as she pushed a little deeper into Nikki. She craved the power it gave her feeling this woman under her. Knowing she could do anything to her and Nikki would obey her.

Nikki slid it in further. It went in easier each time. A couple more times it was sliding in with no problem. "Oh, Alex, this is so good. So good...."

Alex slowly worked the small dildo in a little further each time. "You like it, huh, being filled in both places. Do you want it a little faster? Hmm?"

Nikki could barely think. She could feel the heat building, starting to spread. "Yes, please." She begged Alex to take her faster. She could feel it coming. It wouldn't be long.

Nikki's shaking body beneath her, told Alex that Nikki was close to orgasm. Her own was building fast as well. "You would do anything for me wouldn't you?"

Nikki nodded.

"Tell me. Tell me I own you."

"Yes, I'm yours. Always, forever…"

Alex pulled out. "Tell me!"

"Yes…please. You own me Alex. I do only what you say." She gasped when Alex plunged back into her.

"You're just about ready to come aren't you, baby? I can feel it building inside you. You can't come yet. I didn't say you could." Alex squeezed her ass hard.

"Oh, please, I'm soon…I…don't know…how much longer….Oh, Alex…"

Alex could feel the tremors starting in Nikki's body. "Ah, ah…I didn't hear you ask permission."

"Please Alex, please can I come?" Nikki would do anything to come.

"I can feel you shaking…your body needs it so badly. Tell me what you want. Tell me." She pulled out of her, hovering just at her opening.

Nikki would do anything to get more. "I want more Alex, please…more…."

"More what… Tell me!" She slapped Nikki's left cheek, playfully once then harder a second time. "I love this tattoo on your ass. I want you to get another next to the symbol. I think my badge would be cool, that way I can go everywhere with you. Now baby, tell me what you want!"

"Fuck me, Alex, please."

Alex still denied her what she craved.

"Where Nik, where?" She slapped her harder this time, too hard. She left behind a red imprint of her hand. Alex knew there would be bruises in the morning. She didn't care.

Then Alex slapped her so hard that Nikki knew. She knew this was meant to be a lesson, a lesson not to disobey her. She was so excited though, she didn't care. "Fuck my ass! Oh… God… Alex… Yes…" Nikki pulled the sheets so hard with her fists that she heard the fabric ripping. It was then that it hit her.

Leaning over her, Alex whispered into her ear as she plunged into her. "Come for me, baby."

The orgasm that ripped through her was like nothing she'd ever felt. She heard screaming and realized it was her screaming for Alex to take her faster and harder. Nikki felt a second one hit just as she collapsed onto the bed.

It had been about control and domination…submission and subservience. Nikki knew Alex wanted her to know who was in charge. To know who was master and who should remember their place. Alex wanted her to know she had no choice in the matter but to submit to her and do as she was told.

†

Total domination over Nikki was all that mattered now. Alex was no longer in control, just as she could no longer control her urges when it came to other women tempting her.

†

The next morning as Nikki put Alex's clothes into the washing machine, she found it. It was a small piece of paper with a phone number and a name on it. A woman's name… Several thoughts ran through her mind, none of them good. She was afraid that Alex was cheating on her.

There was of course the other time that Nikki thought she was, but Alex had made her believe that it was not true. Was it though? Was she sleeping with someone else? What was she going to do? Nikki didn't dare question her on it. Was it worth the fight? Was it worth the consequences?

Nikki had to think. With Alex still asleep upstairs, Nikki had the peace she needed. What was she going to do about Rory? Was it such a short time ago that Rory had kissed her? It was the same day Rory let her know she knew what Alex was capable of doing.

"No, she wouldn't cheat on me. Besides, she had me right where she wants me. Last night had been about control and domination. I can't do a thing but submit to her every whim," she told herself.

She couldn't walk away, she had nowhere to go, besides she hated being alone. It was actually one of the things that scared her most. Being alone caused her as much fear as knowing what Alex would do if she ever tried to leave.

Several hours later Alex found Nikki sitting in front of the fireplace with a cup of tea, reading a book. Running her fingers through Nikki's hair, she kissed her on the lips.

"Mornin' babe, you look good this morning." She kissed her again. "I think we both needed that last night, with everything that's been going on. Did you eat breakfast yet?"

Nikki looked up at a freshly showered Alex, with her blonde hair wet and slicked back. She suddenly remembered all the good times they had shared. "God, I love you." She pulled Alex down for another kiss.

Breakfast, as well as thoughts of Rory and the note in Alex's pocket, were all forgotten when Alex led her back up the stairs to the bedroom where they had breakfast of a different sort.

†

Nikki couldn't bring herself to ask about the note she'd found. Nor did she question Alex on nights that she came home late. Nikki only knew that whatever was transpiring was helping in Alex not losing her temper. Her friendship with Rory continued. Alex hadn't scared her away.

Alex fawned over Nikki, making her every wish come true. There had been no more lost tempers, no more punishments. Alex was even entertainingly funny when Rory and Lydia came for dinner. Someone looking in from outside would have thought she was a completely different person.

Something was making Alex behave. Nikki didn't care. She only wanted peace. Not once did she question the calmness. Each night of the past two weeks, Alex brought their lovemaking to new heights. Nikki relished in the new feelings Alex brought out of her.

Others knew that deep inside Alex was the same person, they were just waiting for her to revert to her old behavior. Scott was waiting for her to slip at work and Kirstin was waiting for another visit revealing more than she could imagine. Rory and Liz spoke with Nikki every day, watching for any sign the abuse was starting again.

Three more packages mysteriously appeared, all to Nikki, yet they yielded no more clues as to who was sending them. Mahoney convinced the FBI that they didn't need to get involved. He wanted his own people to handle this. He didn't want his officer's dirty laundry hung out to dry for everyone to see. He also didn't want the personal lives of certain officers too closely scrutinized, which was sure to happen if the outside started looking in.

Even without talking about it, he knew Alex was having issues at home. Mahoney was sure the packages didn't help matters now that Nikki seemed to have become the main focus. He knew Alex well enough to know that she wanted to handle it on her own.

The last of the three packages arrived that morning. The only thing that was in the box was a picture. It was a picture of them as Alex made love to Nikki on a lounge chair on the back deck of their house. The picture was taken right at dusk. Whoever it was must have used a telephoto lens. The picture was very close-up. Alex informed Scott that she remembered hearing no one near their property, that it could have been taken on a motion sensor timer and the person came back later for it.

That Sunday morning they also got another lead. A ten-year-old neighborhood child noticed something out of place. Luckily for them, the kid awakened early and went onto the front porch to play. He was old enough to know that there was something going on with Alex and Nikki when the officers had come to ask his father if he had seen any strangers in the area. Seeing the box on their porch and knowing there was no delivery on Sundays, he went inside for his father, who in turn immediately called Alex.

Alex and Scott sat at their desks contemplating the new information. Alex was sure it was a man. However, Scott kept reminding her it could be a woman as well. They tried to trace the items back to the stores that carried them. Unfortunately, the items were quite popular and could be found anywhere.

Alex threw the autopsy reports she'd been reading onto her desk. She watched as they scattered all over. Her desk looked like a disaster zone, which everyone took as a bad sign. She was always the person who yelled at the rest of them to clean up their messes. Looking up, she glared at Scott as he cleared his throat. "Yesss…you wanted something?"

"PMS?" As the words left his lips, he regretted them. Sometimes things just slipped out. Scott heard her growl as she stood. Leaning across the desk, Alex stared right at him.

She pushed away from her desk, knocking her chair sideways in the process. "Tell me Scott, did Tessa want any more children, or is one enough?" Alex put her hands on her hips. "If not, I assume there was something you wanted."

"Well, I was just thinking that out of all the females we interviewed, only two pop out as being possibilities." He threw the two files on her desk and sat back down.

Alex stood waiting to hear the rest. When he wasn't forthcoming, she prodded him. They played this a little game once in a while. "Okay I'll bite, which two?"

She didn't bother to pick up the files. She wanted to hear his theories first. She calmly picked up the chair and sat back down.

Scott picked up the two files. He set one in front of her, the other he put on his desk out of her reach.

Alex smiled at his maneuver. "Go on…"

"Well the first one I think you'll really like. It's the file on Ann. I read back through the file we have on her. I believe she has knowledge of everything in the notes sent to you and Nikki. She could've been following you around and we would have thought nothing of it. Remember when we ran into her a couple of times at really bizarre places?"

She skimmed through the file. Closing it, Alex looked up at him. "Shit, I didn't even think about that. She did show up in some weird places during the past couple of years. We should bring her back in and cook her some more. Okay, who is the second person?"

She had an inkling she wasn't going to like this, not one little bit.

Hesitantly he picked up the second file. "Alex, you're not going to like this one, but she is the second best possible candidate. The third I ruled out completely. Actually, there was a fourth, an old girlfriend of yours. I ruled her out as well. She overdosed last year."

He handed the file to her.

"Who was the third?" she asked, still looking up at him. She set the file on her desk, not looking at it yet.

Scott had the good sense to take a step back. "Nikki." He took another step back as she sprang out of her seat.

"What?! Are you fucking nuts?! Don't you even dare insinuate that she could have anything to do with this shit! What the hell are you thinking? Have you lost your marbles?"

Scott held up his hand to stop her tirade. "Alex, I'm just doing my job. Okay? Just calm down, why don't you look at the second file?" She was already in a mood and Scott was afraid the other folder might push her over the edge.

She looked at the name on the file, then back up at him. "You've GOT to be fucking kidding me! Is this your idea of some sick joke? If it isn't well, let's just say I hope you enjoy your hospital stay."

"Alex, I thought long and hard about this. I'm sorry, but I had to put that file together. Do you want me to do my job or not? This person has personal knowledge of *everything* that has been in the letters, as well as all the items that have been sent. That's all I'm doing with regards to that file - *my* job. I care a great deal about you and Nikki."

He picked up his coffee cup and went to refill it. He wanted to give her a few moments to calm herself down.

When he returned Alex still hadn't touched the file. He sat behind his desk, out of arm's reach. She looked at him. "Shit, you're right, aren't you?

Well let's take a look at *my* file." She opened the file and read through it.

When she was done, she walked to Scott's desk and threw the file down. "Good job. I didn't do it. So, that leaves us with Ann. Let's go with that angle for now. Unfortunately, we're going to have to get her to confess to it, because nothing we have ties back to her or anyone else for that matter."

Scott had thought about why they shouldn't bring her in for questioning. Now it was just a matter of convincing Alex. "I think we should hold back for a little while. Whoever is doing it is slipping. They delivered it on a Sunday which was a huge gamble because everyone is home. I believe that they're going to slip again. If we drag her in here now and it is her, she'll know we're watching her."

Alex sighed. "True, maybe we should hold off. We'll just watch her very close from this point on. I think Nikki felt better this morning knowing we might have a break. I don't think I'll tell her that we suspect Ann though."

Alex picked up her jacket, heading toward the door. "I sure as hell won't tell her you think that I'm a suspect too. Let's grab some lunch."

†

Nikki's Monday morning was chaotic as usual. She was looking forward to her lunch with Rory. When Mark called a department head meeting first thing in the morning, it blew her whole day out of the water. He wanted to let them know his idea to open an office in L.A. and he wanted their input. She was interested in getting Rory's opinion of the new office. She also wanted to talk to her about what had happened that weekend.

Before their food arrived, she told Rory about the boy seeing the box on the porch. "Alex thinks she knows who it was, but doesn't want to discuss anything yet."

Rory raised an eyebrow. She was still suspicious of Alex. Instead of voicing her concern to Nikki, Rory just smiled and offered her support. "I'm very relieved that it might finally be wrapped up. I know that you've felt like someone was always watching you. Hopefully now it will be over."

"Actually it's more like stalking. I felt as if eyes followed me everywhere I went. I truly hope it's over."

Rory felt the need to change the subject. She brought up her uncle's plan. "It's going to be quite a bit of hard work setting up the new office. Plus we have to train all of the new people."

"I know. It's going to require the two of us going out there for at least a month." Nikki was afraid Alex would throw a fit when she found out.

"Is Alex going to be okay with us going to L.A. together?" Rory didn't want to cause any problems. It was her fear that it would set Alex off on another one of her rages.

Nikki had been thinking of nothing else since the meeting. Unsure on how to break the news to Alex, she thought of having an impromptu dinner that evening. That way they could already be discussing it, and then break it to her.

"Can you and Lydia come for pizza tonight?" She crossed her fingers.

Rory smiled. She'd been thinking the same thing. "I think that would be a perfect idea. That way it won't seem like such a big deal."

Nikki laughed. "Am I that transparent? I must be pathetic, huh?" She sat back as the waitress cleared their dishes away. "God, that was good. I have been craving that dish for more than a week."

"Well, you sure cleaned the plate. I, however, cannot eat a dish called 'Rattlesnake Pasta' even though I know it is made with chicken. I'm sorry but I just can't. I'll stick with my burger and fries."

Rory set her napkin on the table then pushed back a little to give herself some breathing room. "Damn, I'm full."

Nikki looked at her watch. "Yeah we should probably get back. I still have several more nightmares to clear up before leaving today. Why don't you bring the truck around and I'll pay the bill?"

"K…I'll meet you out front."

✝

Another woman exited moments later. Contemplating what to do next, she watched them pull away from the parking lot. The dark shadow thought all the gifts she'd been sending would have made Nikki fear everyone and anyone, not trusting

125

herself to go out in public because she was being watched at all times.

The woman lurking always out of sight knew she would win in the end. At any cost. She laid out the plan in her warped mind then went on about her life as if nothing was amiss.

Chapter Four

Betrayal Most Complete

Six weeks of hard work behind them, the satellite office was ready to open. Many long nights and weekends were spent working out the intricacies. Nikki and Rory spent nearly all of their waking hours working together. Neither of them saw their girlfriends much.

To Lydia it didn't matter. She'd found someone to settle down with and was ready to call things off with Rory. Alex was another matter. She didn't like the amount of time the two were spending together. She also didn't like how close they were becoming. Alex's inner demons told her Nikki had feelings for Rory.

Not able to accomplish certain items on the phone, the pair had to fly to L.A. several times. On the final trip, Alex demanded to accompany them. She suspected Rory of trying to steal Nikki away.

Rory noticed a slight difference in Alex's behavior during the previous few weeks. Alex stuck with Nikki like a second skin, never letting her out of her sight. During the trip, Alex found fault with every decision Nikki made. She didn't like the hotel. She didn't like the restaurants where they ate. It was never ending.

Alex went as far as making them return to the hotel when the three decided to attend the fireworks display to ring in the New Year. Alex felt it better that they watch them from the restaurant in the hotel instead of being in a large crowd of thousands. She didn't want to take a chance of losing sight of Nikki. Or worse, someone finding it necessary to touch her girlfriend inappropriately. Alex insisted it was bound to happen when you had such a large crowd of drunks all in one place.

The last straw was on the final morning when, in front of Rory, Alex criticized the clothes Nikki had put on earlier. By that time, she had listened to enough of Alex's tirades. Rory promised herself that once they were home, she was going to talk to Nikki about it. She didn't want to confront Alex, fearing Nikki would suffer the fall out. She'd already pushed the issue enough on the morning of their return.

Holding Nikki by the arm, Alex pushed her toward the elevator. "Those cargo shorts are too baggy and that top shows way too much cleavage. It makes you look like a hooker. Go back up to the room and change. We'll meet you in the restaurant for breakfast." Alex gave her a rough shove.

Rory was angry. "Nikki, hold up. I think you look great. I don't see a need for you to change." Her remarks earned her a deadly glare from Alex.

Even though Rory had told her she looked great, Nikki returned to their room to change. She knew the consequences if she didn't. Slowly she walked to the elevator and waited. Looking behind her, she saw Rory watching her retreat.

"It's better this way," she whispered to herself.

Rory still couldn't comprehend why she'd changed. Was Nikki that fearful of Alex? Wanting only to give her self-confidence, Rory feared she'd only made matters worse. The entire trip home Alex never said more than two words to Rory.

Monday morning found Rory at her desk waiting for Nikki. She'd arrived several hours early to complete as much as she could, before Nikki was due to arrive. When Nikki passed through her office to get to her own, Rory planned to corner her then.

What exactly she was going to say, she wasn't sure. She just knew that something had to be done. "Hopefully she'll have enough faith in me to accept help and not hate me instead."

Driving to work, Nikki's mind replayed her weekend. "Thankfully Rory will have a lot on her plate to take care of this morning. We rarely see one another on Mondays. It would just make it so much easier."

Nikki wanted to just brush the past two weeks under the carpet. Rory spent her Mondays finalizing the paperwork for any project they were currently working on and gathering their department's payroll numbers for submission. She'd go to each department retrieve the data then update her project files. Knowing Rory would bring up what had happened in L.A., she just didn't want to deal with it.

In addition, she didn't want Rory to see the bruise on her neck. As Nikki pulled into the parking lot, her hand went to the side of her neck as she remembered. "Oh God, Saturday night…"

✝

By the time they arrived home from the airport Saturday night, Alex was in a volatile mood. She felt Rory's behavior had confirmed her suspicions— they were having an affair. She would have to put a stop to it right then and there. Nikki was hers and hers alone.

Alex knew she'd have to be careful though. She didn't trust Rory one little bit. She would have to remind her lover who she belonged to, while at the same time stop Rory from sniffing around Nikki.

That night she did just that. Alex reminded Nikki of who she belonged to. She had brutally taken her, all the while having one hand around Nikki's throat.

Nikki didn't try to fight back. She let Alex do what she needed to. As long as she was taking it out on her, Nikki knew she wouldn't go after anyone else. That scared her more, especially knowing what Alex was capable of.

Later that night Nikki stepped into the shower, she let the water wash across her, washing away the terror. She stood under the water for several long moments before starting to clean off her bruised body. Upon washing her pubic area, she winced.

Looking down she found blood. Leaning her head against the shower wall, her body shook as she tried holding back the tears. Alex had been rough last night as she had rammed her whole arm into her repeatedly, but Nikki prayed she wouldn't leave any evidence of it. Alex had been drinking again. When she was drunk, she didn't know her own strength.

I don't know how much more I can take of this. We were doing so well. Now we're back to square one. This has to end. She needs to get help, we both do. It gets better for a few months then it starts again. Oh God, what am I going to do? She cried silently.

Finished showering, she stepped out to dry herself. Looking up from the bruises on her body, she looked in the mirror. There on her neck was Alex's hand print. She gasped, knowing how visible it would be. Hopefully some of it would fade by Monday morning.

Nikki couldn't let Alex see the bruises either. As she crawled back into bed, Alex sat up, holding her head. Nikki ran her fingers through Alex's hair to pull it away from her face. She then gave Alex the bottle of water and aspirin that she brought from the kitchen before she'd taken her shower.

Alex downed the tablets and most of the bottle of water. "Damn, who stomped on my head?" She lay back, gently putting her head on the pillow.

Nikki lay next to her, kissing her on the cheek. "I think the name was Mr. Scotch. The aspirin should kick in real soon. Just go back to sleep, it's late at night or very, very early. All depends on how you look at it."

As Nikki got up to shut off the light, Alex grabbed her arm. "Aren't you going back to sleep too?"

She laid her hand on top of Alex's. She looked from their entwined fingers to the ring on her hand, then to the tattoo on Alex's arm. She traced it up Alex's arm with her finger. "I was going to turn off the light. That was all. I'll just be a second, okay?"

Her eyes traveled to Alex's bare chest, landing upon the ring through her left nipple. After all this time, she still couldn't believe Alex had done that. She did like it though. She found it extremely sexy.

Letting go of Nikki's arm, she pulled the sheet up over her naked body. "While you're up, turn the heat down. It's getting hot in here." She then rolled and went back to sleep.

Nikki turned off the light and crawled back into bed. Lying awake for another hour, she contemplated her actions, or lack thereof. She knew she should fight back, that she should walk away from her, but she just couldn't. Knowing what Alex would do, she couldn't chance it.

She wanted no one else hurt. Especially now, knowing how Alex felt about Rory. She would blame her for Nikki leaving her. Alex would then go after her. She could never bring that judgment down upon anyone. Rolling away from Alex, Nikki thought Monday was going to come way too soon.

✝

She was right, it came way too early. She should've just called in sick. Waking up that morning, she found the bruises had hardly faded during the past twenty-four hours. Nikki opened the door, taking a deep breath and was momentarily startled to find Rory at her desk so early.

That was the opportunity that Rory needed. Stepping out from behind her desk, she took Nikki's arm. Leading her into Nikki's office, Rory closed and locked the door behind them. Turning, she saw the bruise on Nikki's neck. Rory's anger boiled over, leaving her speechless and motionless. She was too afraid to move, all she wanted to do was take Nikki in her arms and never let go. Closing her eyes, Rory took a deep breath, trying to wash some of it away.

Her hand moved from Nikki's arm to her caress her face. It then traveled to the bruise, lingering there. Rory didn't realize her fingers were massaging Nikki's neck until she saw her close her eyes then lean into the caress. The anger resurfaced.

Nikki was afraid to meet Rory's eyes, afraid of what she would see there. She didn't want to see the disappointment.

Rory gently lifted Nikki's face so their eyes would meet. "Nikki, do I even need to ask who did this?" She lowered her head until their foreheads touched.

Nikki put her hands on Rory's hips. "It's nothing really, just an accident."

Rory's free arm made its way around Nikki's waist. "I wanted to talk to you about Alex. Seeing this bruise this morning causes me even more concern. I care about you and I'm tired of seeing you hurting whether it is physically or mentally."

She pulled their bodies tighter together so Nikki couldn't pull away.

"Rory you don't need to be concerned. I can handle Alex. She loves me. Sometimes she just drinks a little too much, gets a little too rough, or lets jealousy get to her. That's all. She would truly never harm me."

Reaching down Rory pulled Nikki's face back up to meet hers. "That's a crock of shit and you know it. She's abusive and she's obviously not going to stop until she gets help. If you don't leave her at least see to it that she gets some help."

Nikki tried to turn away but Rory held on. "Please, Rory don't…"

Rory knew Nikki was almost at the breaking point. "I would never hurt you. Please don't pull away."

She felt so good in Rory's arms yet Nikki knew it couldn't be. It could never be home. It could never be anything. Even though her body craved the attention, nothing could exist between them.

"Please Nikki, let me in. I do care."

She then did what felt natural, what she'd wanted to do since she first laid eyes upon Nikki. Rory kissed her as a lover would, letting all her feelings pour through her lips into the smaller woman.

That was all it took. She broke. "Yes… But she does love me. She's just protective and possessive. She likes things her way."

Knowing she didn't want to hear the answer, Rory asked anyway, "What happened to cause this bruise?"

Nikki looked away, ashamed.

"Nikki, please, what did she do?" She had an idea what it was. Rory's body tensed.

"Rory, I…" She took a deep breath. "She had her hand there, while she…oh, God…" Nikki's body gave out. She sank against Rory, sobbing. "She wanted to make sure I didn't put up a fight."

Rory's fear became reality with those words. She had feared Alex would lose control and eventually rape her when she said no. Rory's body shook. "Nikki, has she done this before?" She felt Nikki nod her head.

"You need to leave her now and you need to press charges. I can help you. Please, Nikki, you need to do this before it's too late."

She felt Nikki's body start to shake. Rory realized she was shaking with laughter. However, it was not normal laughter. It verged on maniacal.

"It's already too late, I made my bed. I now have to pay the piper. You can't help me. I won't allow you to help me. I don't want you hurt."

Rory's hand caressed Nikki's hip as they stood sharing their hearts' words. "I can take care of myself, Alex doesn't scare me. Having you at her mercy though terrifies me. You have to leave her."

"I can't! Don't you understand anything? I can't leave her. Never!" Nikki pulled away, storming across her office to the windows that overlooked the city. She was afraid of this happening. This was why she could never let anyone in. Nikki felt Rory walk up behind her and put her arms around her waist.

"Why? Why can't you leave her? What terrifies you so much?"

Nikki laid her hands over Rory's. "The bottom line is I will never leave her." Leaning her head back, Nikki rested it on Rory's shoulder. "Why did you have to make me feel again? I can't tell you why. All I can say, is I will never leave her, ever. I love her. That is all you need to know. Please ask no more."

Nikki sighed, resting her mind a moment. "I can't take a chance ever. Can you understand that? Alex is my world and I will stick with her. I'm sorry, Rory, truly sorry."

"Nikki, please, I can help you." She leaned to kiss the bruise on Nikki's neck.

Nikki pulled just out of Rory's reach. "No, Rory. I can't allow that, ever. I'll never leave her. This weekend she was just a little jealous was all. You can't ever say anything to Alex. Please. You have no idea what she is capable of." Nikki turned in Rory's arms.

"I have some idea what she is capable of. I see it in every bruise, in every broken bone and in your eyes that hold the fear. Do you think those eyes could ever show love for someone other than

Alex…Someone that could take you far away from her?"

Nikki didn't dare answer her honestly. She knew of only one answer. "No. I can love only Alex. Nothing else can ever be."

Rory looked at Nikki. "You know what? You don't lie very well."

Nikki pulled back from her, turning to look out the windows once more. "I shouldn't have even let you in this much. It'll only hurt more in the end. I'm sorry, Rory. There's nothing that can be done."

Nikki was so lost in her own thoughts she never heard Rory leave her office. Turning, she found she was alone. It was then that she collapsed, falling into her chair. Head in her hands she sobbed. Nikki knew she'd lost something precious. She'd lost any chance she might have had for a way out, when Rory walked out her door. "Oh God, what have I done?"

†

The heartache set in as Rory watched Nikki pull back into herself. She suddenly felt cold, and lonely. Never before in her life had Rory felt this way. She had never before cared as much as she did now. There had always been another woman waiting.

Even through her relationship with Lydia, there had been others. Rory knew there could never be another, that she would now spend her life alone. She had lost her heart to this beautiful, tormented woman before her.

137

Rory knew what she had to do. She knew Nikki had feelings for her. What she had to do would make Nikki end up hating her. It had to be done. She had no choice. Pulling her cell phone from her waist, she left the office without saying another word. Rory dialed a number that she fortunately never had to use very often.

A gruff female voice answered. "Blackhawk."

"Lillith, your services are required. Where are you?"

"I'm in Lethbridge. Today was Haley's funeral. This sucks."

Rory heard voices in the background. Lillith was obviously still at the funeral.

"Shit, I forgot today was her funeral. How's Remmy holding up? Did you talk to her father?"

Haley, an old friend of theirs, who worked as a corrections officer, had been brutally murdered.

"She's horrible. Yeah, I talked to him. I told Taylor to call us if he needs us." Lillith slammed the truck door as she started the engine.

"Good, thank you for doing that. We'll talk more when you get here. Now back to business. I'll send you the address of where I need you to be."

"I'll be there in two."

With that, the line to Rory went dead as another phone dialed an old friend for a favor. Lillith wanted to arrive as fast as possible and he was the fastest in the air.

†

Walking into his office, Rory sat in the chair across from her uncle. Mark suspected his niece had feelings for Nikki. He saw it in her eyes every time she looked at her. So, it came as no surprise when his niece walked into his office, shutting the door behind her.

"Uncle Mark we need to have a serious talk about LA."

†

Two hours later Rory dialed a number that in the end would change the course of many lives. She had already spoken with her uncle and everything was set on that end.

Rory laid out the plan for Lillith, who had arrived via helicopter moments before. The large woman sitting beside Rory was someone only called on as a last resort. Lillith growled with anger as Rory told her about the person they were meeting up with.

The number connected. Rory could hear resentment in the voice of the woman who answered. "Yeah, what do you want?"

"Meet me at the Whitehouse. No arguments. I'll be there in thirty minutes. If you're not there I'll find you." She disconnected without another word.

Turning to Lillith, Rory smiled. "The game is afoot Watson!" Then she laughed. She had never wanted Nikki to hate her. Now there was no other option. It was ludicrous.

"I feel you are enjoying this almost too much, my old friend. However if there is no other option to be taken…"

"Oh please. Tell me you're not looking forward to this too. It's good to see you on the right side of life now."

"Yes. It has been a long road for the both of us. For me though, there is no absolution."

"Did you send the birthday gifts to Dakota and Kia?"

Lillith graced Rory with a rare, full smile. "Yes. It does not atone for the devastation I brought to their lives. If I am allowed to go back and change only one of my many regrets, I wish for it to be the afternoon I took away their mother."

Rory laid her hand upon Lillith's thigh. "Don't do this to yourself. You've changed since then, doing more good in the past three years to more than make up for your past."

"No. No amount can do that. Even when Ayasha called me last year with the news, I felt no relief."

Rory shook her head in disbelief. "I still can't believe it. Mika…it still feels so unreal. If I had kids, I don't think I could've stayed away from them like she did for six years. I have to commend Mika for what she endured."

Cold eyes misted over, behind the Ray-Bans™. "As long as I breathe I will never understand why they forgave me."

"Because my friend…you are a good person. Under that 'don't fuck with me' crust, you deserve to be forgiven. Mika knew that, as well as Ashley. That is why they chose to lay the past to rest and move on. You must do the same. What you need is a nice girl to settle down with."

Lillith closed her eyes a moment. "That will never happen. I will not allow another to suffer for my past indiscretions."

Pulling into the parking lot, Rory turned off the ignition. "We'll discuss this further at a later time."

The familiar truck was already parked, its driver inside the lodge. Rory set her head on the steering wheel, drawing a deep breath. "I hate this, Lil, but it has to be done. I never wanted to walk this line again. Oh God, I fucking hate what I have to do."

Rory laid her head back against the seat.

Lillith had been with Rory through the rough times and the good ones. Her friend knew what she was capable of. Lillith could be the most tender soul or the devil herself. Lillith reflected on those times for a moment. "It sounds to me as if there is no other way."

Rory looked at the woman sitting next to her. It had been several years since she had truly looked at her. Every time was like a new experience. Rory knew she was capable of taking on the best and winning. She'd never met another woman like Lillith Blackhawk. Standing at six-six and built like a professional wrestler, she pulled off the aura of danger well. That she was almost full-blooded Native-American only added to the allure.

They had met many years ago on the wrong side of the law, becoming instant friends. Trying the relationship route, they decided they made better friends. Yes, they occasionally did end up in bed together. They both knew it was only a means to an end.

"What are you thinking about?" Lillith asked, already knowing the answer.

"Just thinking how we ended up best friends and occasional fuck-buddies instead of in a serious relationship."

"We both know why." She patted Rory's thigh.

"Yeah, we're both volatile bastards...." Rory laughed though her heart hurt. "I guess it's time." Closing her eyes, she closed her heart once more.

Looking up at the lodge, Rory growled. It came from deep within. This needed to be done. "For Nikki..." With that, she let the anger within her loose. Her eyes turned the color of coal and she pushed her soul to the farthest depths of her being. With it, she pushed away all of the love she held for Nikki.

Opening her door, she stood. "Showtime...."

Before closing the truck doors each of them retrieved their weapons from under their seats, securing them before entering the lodge.

†

Nikki sat looking out the conference room window at the landscape, knowing something was wrong. "I just talked to Alex, so everything's okay with her. Still I can't shake this feeling of dread. I just wish this meeting would start."

In the pit of her stomach, something was very, very wrong. Nikki had been waiting ten minutes when the others finally walked in.

†

Alex was lost in thought when she heard the cabin door close and lock. The locking mechanism clicking jump-started her nerves. Turning, she saw that one of the women she knew, and the other, she did not want to know. The woman was huge, a mountain. Something was very wrong and it was two against one. Alex felt confident she could handle anything Rory could throw at her until that moment. She now felt fear sliding in.

"Hello, Alex. We need to have a little chat about someone very close to both of our hearts." Rory watched as Alex's fear turned to rage.

"I fucking knew it! I knew there was something going on with you two. So, you're here to tell me you're taking her away from me? I don't think so. She'll never leave me! Why are you really here?"

She stepped back a few feet to put more space between them.

Rory's features turned feral. "To deal."

She looked at Lillith then walked to the windows on the wall facing the lake. "How would you like to make a deal with the devil herself, Alex?"

Alex growled. "Fuck you!" She kept her eyes on the mammoth woman in front of her. She didn't trust taking her eyes off her. Knowing that she would never make it to her gun in time, Alex stood very still, not wanting to provoke *it*.

Rory snarled. "Sorry, I don't fuck animals."

Lillith snickered at Rory's words. Both Lillith and Rory thought of Alex as their prey. Slowly Rory walked to the windows facing the lawn on the opposite side they had come in on. The maneuver placed Alex between the two of them with her back to Rory. The detective didn't realize what Rory had done until it was too late.

Rory knew the idiot wouldn't be able to take her eyes off Lillith, making her job even easier. Nodding to the other woman, Lillith took a step toward Alex. Out of reflex, Alex stepped back.

Within a click of a second Rory pulled her gun and moved in behind Alex. She had her by the neck, the gun to her temple. "Deal or fucking say hello to Hades!"

Alex weighed her options. She, however, let ego reign over common sense. "Why would I want to do that?"

"Because if you don't, I will take her away from you and don't think for one minute that I am afraid of you. Between my friend here and me, we have many ways of making you comply or if necessary disappear." She pushed the gun a little harder into Alex's temple. She felt Alex's body shake with laughter.

"Oh? No one can make a cop just disappear. No one is that good." Alex knew she was pushing her luck. She just couldn't stop herself.

Rory's hand tightened around Alex's neck. "I wouldn't push her if I were you. She can kill you in the blink of an eye and I don't know if I would stop her. I'm going to give you two options. Option one: I walk away from Nikki and in the process, I make it so she hates me for the rest of her life. You treat her with the love and respect she deserves and never lay another hand on her. If you do, we'll know and you'll be very sorry. Option two: I take her away from you. At that point you can go on with your life or you can have a little accident."

"Either way she'll hate you, you know that don't you?" Alex said, sneered. "I'm not sure I understand why you would risk that."

Rory put her lips against Alex's ear. "For something I don't think you can understand. For her happiness. She loves you for some reason, which I cannot begin to fathom. I am willing to walk away from her, but only on that one condition." She let go of Alex's neck, moving the gun from her head.

"So, do we have a deal?" She took a couple of steps back from Alex. Rory knew Alex was not stupid. She would never give up Nikki. Alex would do whatever she had to do to keep her.

Alex turned to look Rory in the eyes. She felt nervous turning her back on the other woman but she wanted to see the look on Rory's face. "Option one. You leave town and never look back. And she hates your fucking guts forever." With the last sentence a new sneer crossed Alex's face.

Rory stepped to within inches of Alex. "Done. However, my friend will be keeping an eye on you. If you step over the line, you will be meeting up with the devil herself. Got it?"

Alex looked at the woman in question. She had never met anyone like her. She was taller than Alex and much wider. Her tan was much darker than anything Alex could ever acquire. She envied her for that. Her long black hair was pulled back into a tight braid that was long enough to touch her ass. The eyes really stunned her. Yet they terrified her at the same time. Where she thought the woman would have black eyes, there were unbelievable pools of blue. Not just blue though, they were translucent, almost crystalline in appearance.

From what she saw in those eyes, she knew this woman was capable of killing. She would most definitely not let her step out of line. Alex knew she would have to be very careful. She would have to behave.

She turned back to Rory. "Deal...." Then she walked out the door.

"Lil, you'll need to be very careful with her. She's a sneaky bitch. Check in on her at intervals as you see fit. I also give you permission to do whatever you feel is warranted. I don't trust her, not one little bit. Let's go, I have a meeting to get to."

They watched Alex pull away as they opened the truck doors. "When do you leave for L.A.?"

Rory fastened her seatbelt, contemplating the upcoming meeting. "I leave in the morning. Lydia will be remaining here. She finally found someone to settle down with and I'm happy for her."

"What about you, why can you not be happy? I have known you for many years now and you deserve to be happy. The truth, Ror...." Lillith already knew the answer but wanted to hear it anyway. Rory needed to admit the truth or it might eat away at her.

"The truth? It's not that easy, not really. The truth though is that nothing matters but her happiness. As long as she's happy, then I'll be happy. Before you ask it... Yes, I love her. I love her more than anything in this world. I have to do this. That is why I will risk her hating my guts for the rest of eternity, because that is how long I will love her. Maybe in the next lifetime, I won't lose her. Maybe..." Rory couldn't stop the tears as she pulled out of the parking lot.

Lillith had known when Rory finally lost her heart, her soul would follow. It tore at her knowing Rory would love Nikki unconditionally and without reservation, yet nothing would ever come of it. Lillith laid her hand on Rory's thigh. They didn't need words to communicate. They had their own code.

†

Pushing away the feeling that something was wrong, Nikki turned to the others upon their arrival. She hated the regular weekly meetings, but these emergency ones were the worst. It usually meant something had blown up. Mark walked into the room and all chairs turned toward him. She didn't like the look on his face. He looked like he had come to send them to their deaths. Nikki had never seen him look so pale.

They discussed all the items they did every week at the normal meetings. Nikki could tell Mark was stalling when he rehashed old items from the last one. When Rory slid through the door and into the seat next to him, she knew why. He'd been waiting for her. He nodded to her as she sat. Nikki saw the eye contact and a shiver ran through her. The sense of foreboding she felt before, came back even stronger.

"Okay, now for new business. As some of you know, our L.A. office will be ready to open in one week. The only thing left to do was to decide who out of our current staff was going to run it. After some consideration, Rory has been chosen for that task. She leaves in the morning."

A stunned hush fell in the room. Nikki felt her lunch coming back up. Quickly excusing herself, she just made it to the bathroom just in time.

A thousand jumbled thoughts ran through her mind. Most of all she felt betrayed. Mark had told her that very morning he hadn't decided who would run the new division. They'd discussed hiring someone from outside the firm for a fresh new approach, now this announcement. Something didn't feel right to her.

Nikki quietly entered her office, closing the door behind her. She was grateful Rory wasn't there to greet her. Nikki knew she'd eventually have to confront her. In the meantime, she needed to get herself together. She heard the outer door close. The quiet knock caused her to jump. It took a moment for Nikki to find her voice.

"Come in." She stood looking out her windows, watching the sun set. This was her favorite time of day. Today it held no pleasure for her. It saddened her that she couldn't feel the warmth inside that the sun's rays always created. Her heart picked up speed. She couldn't find the words to speak what she was feeling. To Nikki, all of Rory's gentle words had been a lie. She let the betrayal guide her actions.

"I guess congratulations are in order. Since you'll be leaving first thing in the morning, please clean your desk out and leave your security badge with the receptionist on the way out."

Turning from the windows, she picked up her bag and started for the door.

"Nikki, can we talk for a moment before you leave?" She held out her hand, motioning for Nikki to sit.

Nikki sat, waiting for Rory to say something, anything that would help her to make sense of what was going on. "Okay, I'll bite. What could we have to talk about at this point?"

Rory pulled the other chair close to Nikki and sat. "I guess I should explain, huh?" She watched as a look of grief overtook Nikki's features.

Rory sat back placing her arms across her chest. She clasped her hands together with her fingertips touching underneath her chin. "I never had any direction in my life. I went from one place and one girlfriend to another. No one in my family thinks I can be trusted with anything and I needed to prove myself. That chance for me was working here. That will only get me so far though. I want to run my own business, to be in charge and have to answer to no one. Then I gave him the idea to open this office in L.A. I can shape it into my own. It will be mine and mine alone. So I nudged him along to open it. I also would much rather live there than here in this tiny town. I know I probably have hurt you. There is nothing I could do about that. You see this place just isn't for me. It's too docile. I need a place filled with nightclubs and women. I'm sorry."

At least some of it was the truth, the rest left her hollow.

Nikki looked up at her. "So, this was just a pit stop for you, on your way to bigger and better things. Well, I'll be damned. Here I thought you actually cared. Huh…go figure." Nikki stood, starting for the door once more.

Rory stood and grasped her arm as she moved by her. "Nikki, I didn't want things to go badly like this between us. I'm sorry. I guess I never figured on you caring about me. I was just looking to have a cool time until this all came to fruition. I truly never meant to hurt you."

Nikki looked down at her arm and then back up at Rory. "Please let go of my arm. You're hurting me." Rory slowly let go of her arm.

Rory raised her hand to wipe the tears from Nikki's eyes but stopped when she saw her flinch. "I would never physically hurt you. You must know that, don't you?" Her heart broke even more when she heard the answer.

"There are worse things than physical pain. So all of this was just a game to you? All the things we talked about, all the things you said? Well, you fooled me. In the end, you're no better than Alex. Yes, she may hurt me, but through everything, she has never broken me, not really, because I've always been able to hold onto something, the tiniest something… Hope. I let you in and now I just wonder how I could have been that stupid." Nikki stopped when she got to the door.

With her hand on the knob she stopped one last time, her head bowed in defeat. "You destroyed that tiny spark of hope that it took me a lifetime to build in a matter of seconds. You should be proud of that. I know Alex would be. You're well on your way to being her replica. Congratulations."

Nikki walked through the door without looking back. Her step faltered several times on the way to her car. Where her strength to continue walking came from, she didn't know. She only knew she had to keep going, that she couldn't let anyone see that anything was wrong.

✝

Nikki left the parking lot, heading toward the lake. She needed to think and try to piece herself back together before heading home. Home to Alex. Home to her life and whatever was to come. She never saw the tail she had. The shadow that would follow her for some time to come, to keep her safe.

She was overlooking the lake, watching the waves roll in when her cell phone rang. Looking at the caller ID, she saw it was Liz. Liz was probably worried about her. Not wanting her to call the house, risking Alex answering, Nikki picked up. She loved her ditzy friend dearly but sometimes she let her mouth rattle on and Nikki didn't want Alex to hear any of what happened today from anyone but her.

Nikki flipped open the phone. "I'm okay, Liz. I was just thrown a little."

"Nikki, come on, don't give me that. I know you started letting her under your skin."

Nikki couldn't stop the laugh that burst free from her. "You have no idea at all. I let her inside. How stupid of me. God, how could I risk everything like that? I must say she's good. She had me completely under her spell. Oh God, Liz…" Nikki set the phone on her thigh and rested her head on the steering wheel.

Several long moments passed. "Liz, you are my best friend. Thank you for listening, but this is my problem not yours. I don't want to put you in the middle of it. I have to get going. I'll talk to you later in the week." Nikki turned the phone off completely.

She had much to contemplate. Betrayal crept into her bones. She never knew she could hurt so much. She wanted to die. She contemplated driving her car into the water and drowning herself.

Nikki opened the car door, got out, and walked to the water's edge. *I guess I could just as easily drown myself. Since I don't know how to swim it would be so easy.* She stood looking out over the water, contemplating what was left of her life.

No, she could do neither of those things. Alex would connect the dots, knowing it had something to do with Rory leaving then she would go after her. Even though Nikki felt betrayed, she still cared for her. She didn't want anyone to get hurt because of her.

✝

Nikki knew her frustration was showing in her voice but she wanted her lunch with Liz to be finished. Liz asked question after question that she didn't want to answer. She saw no point in it.

"Liz…I really don't want to talk about it. I am fine. There are no problems with Alex, there never have been. We have a wonderful relationship. I have no plans on leaving her, ever. She's very good to me. She would never hurt me. As far as the issue with Rory is concerned, we were friends and that is all, nothing more. I'm very happy for her. She deserves her own business to run. She has come a very long way since I've known her. I support Mark's decisions all the way. Now I really have to get back, I have a ton of paperwork to get done today and interviews to set up. I'll talk with you later."

Nikki got up from the lunch table and briskly walked back to her office.

✝

All Nikki wanted was to forget all that had happened. Nikki had come to the conclusion that Rory had only used her to further advance herself. Their friendship had meant nothing to the woman. It had been a month since that horrific day. During that time two things had happened - Alex had a not laid a finger on Nikki and Mark had hired a tall, dark woman as a security guard for the lobby.

Alex tried to be loving and attentive, never so much as raising her voice. Nikki was leery, yet she didn't care, all she knew was that Alex was trying to be the woman she fell in love with.

In time, Nikki knew that the hurt she felt would start to ease. She felt shattered inside and every breath she took made her lungs feel like shards of glass. Nikki wanted nothing more than to get on with life. Alex had been very understanding when Nikki told her that Rory was moving to L.A. Even as Nikki cursed the woman on the inside.

✝

Alex had been cursing Rory as well, but for altogether different reasons. Once she gave the situation some serious thought, she knew she'd been given another chance. This time was different though, because someone would be watching her every step. She would have to be very careful to control her temper. She could not lose Nikki, no matter what.

She felt that Rory's leaving was hurting Nikki more that she would admit. Nikki had become quiet and withdrawn, doing whatever Alex wanted without even a second thought. Alex however, wasn't going to let either of those women get the best of her. "Fuck no...I won't let her, or that mountain of a woman she has watching me, win this war. She may have won that battle, but not the war! Nikki's still mine."

†

The moment Nikki met Lillith, the security guard, she knew there was something different about the reserved woman. She was much larger than Nikki, creating a larger than life aura. Nikki found herself drawn to the woman, even though she rarely uttered more than a few words at a time.

†

Two weeks after first being introduced in the lobby to the stoic security guard, Nikki asked her to lunch. During the meal, Lillith listened intently to her chatter on about nothing in particular. It was what Nikki didn't talk about that interested her the most. Not once did she mention Alex's name during their first lunch together. This was to become their routine most days. Lillith listened as Nikki told her about the project she was currently working on or the latest crisis in Liz's love life. She found Nikki's humor refreshing and sometimes enlightening.

When Nikki felt she needed to censure herself, Lillith made her promise never to do it again.

There were to be no barriers in their friendship. Still though, she held back in regards to Alex.

It was not until a month later when Alex's name first passed Nikki's lips. What Lillith heard angered her, yet no emotion showed upon her face. She remained unfazed as always, biding her time. A week later, she could hold her tongue no longer.

Lillith watched as Nikki gingerly slid in the booth across from her. "Are you sure there is nothing wrong?"

Nikki's hesitation at discussing intimate details of her life with Alex had been so ingrained that the lies covering the truth had become automatic. "Positive. Everything is perfect." She winced as she fully sat on her left butt cheek.

Her lunch companion noticed the pain on her face. Lillith could tell Nikki was hurting. Enough was enough, she could wait no longer. It ate at Lillith's insides that the animal Nikki shared her life with would hurt her. "Nikki…" Lillith studied the table for a moment.

Clearing her throat, she began again. "Nikki, please trust in me. I…" The remaining words stuck in her throat when she looked upon Nikki's face.

Nikki smiled, remembering the night before, as Alex became rougher during the night. Alex had spanked her repeatedly as she lay across her lap. So much so, that Nikki had issues sitting without wincing in pain. Thinking of the night before she thought it was most definitely worth what she was suffering afterward.

Smiling at Lillith, Nikki felt in a naughty mood. "It's not what you might think. Well, actually it is what you might think." She laughed at the look on Lillith's face.

"Well...um..." Lillith felt flustered for the very first time in her sinister life.

"I'm sorry I've embarrassed you." Reaching across the table, she took Lillith's larger hand in hers. Lillith smiled. "That's the first time I've seen you smile. If that is what talking about my sex life does, I'll do it more often. You have a beautiful smile and should do it more often." Nikki had no idea where the words came from.

"No, you have not embarrassed me. I am happy you feel so at ease with me that you are able to trust in me with your innermost feelings. I am honored you feel such." She squeezed Nikki's hand.

"I have no idea why I just said what I did." Nikki giggled. "Oh God...I normally don't giggle either. I don't know what is wrong with me today."

"Maybe you are just happy." Lillith felt slightly nauseous. She couldn't figure out why.

"Possibly...maybe it's the company. Either way, you're right, I do feel happy today. So tell me, anything new on the girlfriend front? Any prospects..."

"As I have told you every day since we met, I am not looking. I have nothing to offer in return."

Nikki released her hand. Wiggling her finger at Lillith, she shook her head. "Oh please, when you least expect it a woman will walk into your life. Then you'll be mooning over her as if she's the best thing since sliced bread. After that the next thing you know we'll be discussing your sex life."

"Whatever you say, I do not feel like arguing with you today." It would do no good to tell Nikki she had already found her and that she belonged to another.

†

It was during their lunches that Nikki was able to escape the reality of life, existing in the world of friendship with Lillith. Each time they spoke, a brick was removed from the wall each of them had erected around their hearts. Never in Nikki's life had she felt the sense of calmness she felt when with Lillith.

Lillith was a friend, a confidant in the true sense of the word. Never once did she step out of line, and show her true feelings. During Lillith's life she had become a master of securing every one of her emotions in a box and hiding the box where it would never be found. Nikki needed a rock in her life to ground her and Lillith was to be that rock, that life preserver thrown to her as the ship was sinking. Nikki however, would never sink on her watch. Lillith would die first before she would ever let that happen.

†

Alex decided that it would be fun to have a big cookout that weekend, inviting everyone they knew, even though it threatened to pour buckets. She would even invite Liz to prove to Nikki that she had changed.

Nikki looked around the kitchen. Almost everything was ready and people would be arriving in an hour or so. She was nervous. This was the first party in quite some time and she wanted everything to be perfect.

It lightly misted as Alex and Scott cooked steaks on the grill. Scott took the opportunity to talk privately to Alex. He'd been watching her closely the past several months. To him she seemed much calmer. Scott knew though it could be camouflage for what was brewing under the surface. He just wasn't sure how to approach the subject, especially seeing the bruise on the side of her face. Tessa always told him the best way was be straight forward, no beating around the bush. He figured he'd go with that.

"Alex, I consider you my best friend so don't bite my head off, but how are things going between you and Nikki? I'm just concerned about the two of you, even though you do seem to be calmer than I've seen you in a while. I also haven't seen you cruisin' any of the rookies. So I was wondering if everything is okay. And why the bruise on the side of your face…" Scott knew he was sticking both feet in it, but he didn't care. He cared about the two of them too much to ignore it any longer.

As Scott grilled Alex, Kirstin did the same to Nikki in the kitchen. The others watched a DVD or played pool in the recently renovated den.

Kirstin leaned back against the sink counter trying to get Nikki to open up. When they arrived, she could see the red puffiness around Nikki's eyes and knew something or someone had upset her. What confirmed her suspicions was when Nikki reached for a platter from the cupboard. When she reached up, the short sleeves of her tee shirt had ridden further up her arms and Kirstin could see the bruising on her right arm. Bruising that matched the same color of the one on Alex's lower left arm.

Now that it was just the two of them in the kitchen, she could directly question her. "Nikki, I care about you very much. I think of you as a sister. Something is up. Talk to me, it will help. I can tell you've been crying and I've seen the bruise on your arm. It seems to me there have been way too many of those. Never before have I stepped in. I've always thought you would handle it. Alex needs help. I'll do whatever I can to help, if you'll let me."

Nikki stopped what she was doing. Kirstin knew, but there was nothing she could do about it. She turned to her, remembering when she had finally done the unthinkable that very morning. Looking into Kirstin's eyes Nikki knew she could tell her anything without being judged. "Kirstin, I don't know what to say. Other than thank you. I know you care about both of us. Things were rough there for a while. Actually they've gotten better now."

How much could she say? She took a leap of faith, knowing it would go no further. "Kirstin, as you know she has a temper. Sometimes it gets away from her, especially when she doesn't get her own way. Things have been getting better though."

Nikki saw the look on Kirstin's face.

"Yes, Alex was jealous of Rory. She was convinced we were having an affair. I would never leave Alex and Rory knew that." Nikki mindlessly wiped off the platter with the dishtowel to clean the dust off.

Something that morning snapped inside her. She felt the emotions surging in her. She didn't know if she could hold it in. Fighting back that morning had felt so good. She finally felt she could stand on her own for the first time in her life. Nikki had no idea where the courage came from, but she wasn't about to question it.

"Nikki, did you have feelings for Rory? I can understand if you did and still do. She seemed like a wonderful woman. I have to ask you though, do you still love Alex?" Kirstin loved both of them and wondered for the hundredth time if the best thing for both of them was just to walk away. Kirstin led Nikki to the chairs around the island to sit down.

"Do I still love Alex? Kirstin, I wouldn't know where to start. Rory knew I would never leave Alex. Then she left for L.A. and informed me that being here had meant nothing to her, that it was nothing more than a bump in the road for her. I still feel like a fool. What I don't understand is Rory could have tried to destroy my relationship with Alex and she didn't. Do I love Alex? Yes. Do I love who she became? No. She is trying though. We still have our rough moments, but we'll get through them. I think every couple has those."

Kirstin wiped the tear from Nikki's face with the back of her hand.

Kirstin couldn't believe Nikki had finally opened up to her. She decided to take a chance and push it a little more. "Sweetie, I know she's hurt you physically. I should've said something before now, so it's my fault also for not doing something. It has to stop before something disastrous happens. Is that what happened this morning? Did she hit you again and you fought back this time? Is that how both of you got the bruises? "

Nikki looked at her arm where she knew the bruise was. Alex had indeed been doing better. She was more loving and hadn't physically touched her until that morning. But whose fault was it that morning? Was it Alex's or was it hers? Alex may have stopped physically bruising her but the mental abuse had continued. It was so subtle at first she didn't even realize it.

It was the little things, like she didn't want what Nikki cooked for dinner, she didn't like the way her clothes fit her, saying they made her look like she had gained a few pounds. Alex had worked later and later the past few weeks then would come home and straight to bed. She was exhausted most of the time. But she was trying and that was all that mattered to Nikki.

Then the domestic bliss ended in a heartbeat. That morning Nikki had pulled out a pair of shorts that she hadn't worn since the year before, finding they were a little snug. They, however, looked really good on her, a little too good. They accented her curves and would've made anyone with sight take a second look at her.

Alex found her looking in the mirror. "Take those off. They make your ass look fat. In fact, take that top off too. It shows off your tits too much. What are you doing, going for the fucking slut look? Oh wait, your slut is in L.A., so it can't be for her. She must have realized you're such a lousy fuck. You couldn't satisfy her in bed, could you? Is that why she left town?" Alex had roughly grabbed her arm.

"So tell me if it's not for her, who is it for? You fuckin' around with someone else?"

All the years of misery came crashing down on her. How dare Alex question her fidelity, her devotion! Had she not remained by her side through all of it? Nikki felt the rage welling up inside of her. It started out as a small voice inside and grew as it left her lips. Alex froze, not knowing what was happening.

Nikki jerked her arm away from Alex. She turned to Alex and felt it bubbling from within. It came out quietly. Alex at first wasn't sure she even heard it.

"Shut up." Nikki looked Alex right in the eyes. Alex grabbed for her arm again. This time Nikki was ready for her. Something deep in her propelled her arm forward, turning her hand into a fist.

Before Nikki knew it, she'd punched Alex in the stomach. She rounded her fist for another blow, before Alex had time to react. The second blow hit her in the face, causing a bloody nose, as she doubled over.

Alex hadn't been expecting it and had no time to prepare for it. She had doubled over from the force of the blow and when the second one hit, it sent her mind reeling as well. Nikki never fought back, never raised her voice.

Nikki was then in Alex's face, the rage clearly showing on her face and in her voice. As each second passed, her voice became louder and angrier. "You don't know what you're talking about! I'm sick of the jealousy. I'm sick of the humiliation. I'm sick of the bruises that I have to hide."

Nikki felt her whole body shaking. "I do love you, Alex. However, I don't know if it's enough anymore. Some days you're not the same woman I fell in love with and other days you are. On those bad days, I don't know you at all. You become someone I don't want to know, that I don't want in my life. I can't go on like this. You terrify me. You shouldn't fear the person you love, Alex. I have never had an affair. I have dedicated myself to you. Can you say the same?" Nikki already knew the answer.

Alex walking away told her everything she needed to know.

✝

Dinnertime the following night found Nikki sitting across the table in the crowded restaurant from Lillith, not Alex. Once again, Alex called her earlier to let her know she wouldn't be home for dinner. So in turn, she had asked the silent and contemplative woman if she had plans for dinner that night.

Nikki wondered for the hundredth time what Alex was really doing. Who was she with? When Alex called her earlier, there was quite a bit of noise in the background. Nikki could have sworn she heard music.

Lillith watched the emotions play across Nikki's face. Knowing there were problems in Nikki's home, she was just unsure as to what extent. She sat silent waiting for Nikki to start the conversation. She wasn't disappointed when Nikki looked up from her plate and let loose her inner turmoil.

Spilling forth were all the fears she had that Alex was cheating on her. Then she confided in the stoic woman having dinner with her, her ultimate secrets. The days and nights of verbal abuse, physical abuse and of acts of betrayal forced upon her by the women in her life.

Nikki couldn't stop. She spewed forth her life with Alex and the few short months of friendship with Rory. Falling from her lips were words of love, hatred, and self-loathing for standing by and never once trying to stop it.

Lillith didn't know where she herself drew her courage from to sit by and listen to all Alex had done to the wonderful, beautiful woman who was her dinner companion. She wanted nothing more at that moment than to hunt down and brutally destroy the bitch. However, she would do no such thing. Instead, she would sit and listen to all that Nikki had to say and what she didn't say with words but with mannerisms.

She however, wouldn't listen to, nor tolerate Nikki putting herself down or insinuating that she deserved what had occurred during the years. Lillith finally spoke up.

Few words were ever needed to convey her feelings. "Nikki, you know by now that I am a woman of few words, so I will not change now. You have never, nor will you ever deserve such things. You deserve the world and someone who would treat you as deserving. Someone… Someone, who would worship the ground beneath you. If you believe nothing else in the world, believe that."

A few silent moments passed as both contemplated Lillith's quiet words. Nikki was startled out of thought by her companion's deep voice once more.

"We have become what I care to think of as very good friends and will remain as such 'til my last breath and beyond, no matter on what path our lives lead us. I will never walk in front of you, or behind you. I will always walk beside you. That I vow to you."

Nikki looked up from the cup of coffee she had silently been stirring, moved beyond any words. What had she just heard? What had Lillith just said? Had she just pledged herself to her? No, it was too much to absorb, too much to bear. No, Lillith could not mean what it sounded like to Nikki. She could never ask Lillith to put her life on hold just to protect her.

Her eyes met Lillith's silent ones, eyes that never once gave away the emotions boiling within. "I am honored. However, I cannot ask that of you, never."

Lillith accepted that at that moment in time, her soul was lost to this woman. She would never, throughout eternity, take back her pledge. "As I was honored to pledge them... Never will the words be taken back."

Chapter Five

Deliverance

Fall was Nikki's favorite time of year. She loved the smell of autumn, the coolness of the evenings. The colors were so brilliant she couldn't find words to describe it. To Nikki, New York was the only place to be that time of year. Seneca Lake was her favorite spot within the state, its foliage breathtaking.

Every year she made the effort to take at least a one-day trip along the lake just as the leaves were turning. Along the way, she would visit some of her favorite wineries. One year Alex went with her, another she took Liz. Several trips she went alone, which Nikki found she didn't mind in the least.

Going alone unfortunately meant no one to share the beauty with. Finding that her office was running smoothly once more, Nikki put in for a vacation. She still couldn't believe her luck when Mark agreed to transferring Liz into her department.

Alex surprised Nikki by requesting a few days off to accompany her. Going a step further, she called ahead for hotel accommodations. Alex willingly shelled out the extra money to book a room at the hotel owned and operated by the largest winery on the lake.

Reserving the best room, Alex requested they have several bottles of Nikki's favorite wine in the refrigerator. As an afterthought, Alex had them add a large basket of assorted treats waiting in the room. With the evenings getting cooler, Alex couldn't wait to snuggle in front of the fireplace in the room.

With an hour left until Nikki arrived home, Alex packed her duffle bag to pass the time. Smiling she pulled the small black velvet box from her dresser that she'd picked up that afternoon. Opening it, she ran her finger over the band. "Beautiful. Just like her."

As she was packing, she added a few special items to play with. She wanted to make this trip very special for Nikki, especially considering the previous several weeks. Each had come home late every night dropping exhausted into bed. It had been more than two weeks since they'd made love and both were more than a little sexually frustrated.

Eyeing the black box on the bed, she picked it up. Nikki defending herself the previous week had thrown her. Alex was still trying to come to terms with it. She'd truly been trying. For the most part, she could control her emotions. That was until two weeks ago when she'd made one of her rare appearances at Nikki's work place. When she had walked through the front doors, Alex realized how long it had been since she was in the building. Alex shivered as she remembered the visit.

✝

Alex knew it would make Nikki happy if she surprised her by taking her to lunch. She was pumped up with adrenalin, having closed all four cases they were working on. Alex was never expecting to find what she came upon in the lobby.

Alex stopped dead in her tracks. There behind the security desk sat her nightmare. Alex felt fear when she'd been shot, but when she met this woman, she felt true fear for the first time. This woman was capable of taking everything away from her.

A sight that terrified her even more was unfolding in front of her. Nikki stood talking and laughing with the same mountain of a woman. She looked like she was even enjoying the woman's company. Standing on opposite sides of the desk, they leaned over with their heads close together.

Something she said to Nikki made her giddy with laughter. Alex watched as the other woman put her hand on Nikki's arm. She did so with such familiarity that Alex almost lost control right there in the lobby.

Waiting a moment for the anger to dissipate, she approached the two. Clearing her throat as she approached, she put her arm around Nikki's waist. Kissing Nikki on the cheek, Alex pulled her tight against her. The move spoke volumes. It screamed that Nikki belonged to her.

Alex met her enemy's eyes. "Hi babe, thought I'd come by and take you to lunch."

Nikki was thrown. Alex never showed up unexpectedly at her office. At least not without it being the result of guilt. "Alex, is everything okay?"

Alex turned to her. "Everything is fine. We wrapped up the last of the paperwork this morning on the last case and I have the rest of the day free. So I thought I would spend it with you. Or did you have other plans for lunch?" She looked at the other woman.

"Nope, no plans, I was just leaving a FedEx package here to be picked up. Alex this is Lillith Blackhawk. Lillith this is…"

Before Nikki could finish, Alex interrupted her. "Hello, I'm Alex, Nikki's wife. It's nice to meet you. How long have you been working here?"

Alex extended her hand. Lillith shook it, squeezing extremely hard, knowing it would get her point across. That she knew what Alex had done. That she was waiting for Alex to slip up once again.

When Lillith stood to shake Alex's hand, she realized how much she towered above both women. Finding it amusing, she laughed aloud. Lillith remembered Alex referring to her as a mountain.

Alex was curious as to what she was laughing at. She looked between the two women. "What? Do I have a booger on my nose?"

This made Lillith laugh harder. "Sorry, I was noticing what a *mountain* I am compared to the two of you." When Alex visibly flinched, she knew her meaning had been received.

Inside, Alex was furious. How dare this woman spy on her! For the most part, she was trying. Plus, who was this woman to judge her? Gut instinct told Alex there was much more to this woman. Outwardly, however, she showed no anger, no fear.

"Well if you're done here, what do you say we go to lunch?"

Over lunch, Alex told Nikki how her morning had gone. The last case they just closed threw their completion rate up a few notches. Knowing she shouldn't ask, Alex couldn't stop herself. "How long has Lillith worked for you? I don't remember seeing her last time I was there." Alex grinned. "And what exactly do the two of you talk about? Anything interesting that I should know about?"

Nikki finished her last bite of salad before answering her. Inside she felt it was none of Alex's business what she and Lillith discussed. Nothing she could do or say was going to scare Lillith away. Nikki knew she'd finally found a friend that Alex couldn't intimidate.

"I think it was about six months ago now. I know she looks a little intimidating but she's a very nice person. Before you ask, yes, she's gay and no, she has never hit on me. She knows I'm already taken. My heart goes out to her. I think she's still in love with her wife, whom she lost several years ago in an accident. We've been to lunch a couple of times. Her wife was who we talked about. I felt like it did her good to talk about it, plus she knows I know something about losing someone. I really felt like it brought her a little peace of mind."

"That's very good of you, sweetheart, to help her like that. I'd say the two of you have become friends then. That's nice, gives her someone to talk to. I was thinking we'd have a nice dinner at home tonight then maybe go see a movie if you'd like."

Alex drained the last of her beer from the bottle setting it down a little harder than she had intended.

The thudding of the bottle wasn't lost on Nikki. Something was bothering Alex. Reaching across the table, she took Alex's hand. "Honey, is something wrong?"

Alex sighed then squeezed her hand. "Nothing, babe, just a little tired I guess. Do you think you could take the rest of the day off?"

Nikki folded her napkin before setting it on the table. "I wish I could, but the first round of budgets are due Friday. I need to put the finishing touches on them. I may be late the next couple of nights, I'm sorry."

Nikki could see the resentment in Alex's eyes. *Shit, here it comes.* She thought Alex would cause a fight, but she surprised her by calmly letting the subject drop.

"I guess we need to get you back at it then, huh?" After throwing money on the table, Alex followed her out of the restaurant.

As she escorted Nikki into the lobby, she could feel Lillith's eyes on her. Kissing Nikki good-bye, she watched her get into the elevator. Walking back across the lobby, Alex turned her head slightly, looking at the woman behind the desk. In that moment, the look of hatred on Lillith's face startled Alex.

"Fuck."

Alex knew she was living once again on borrowed time. She would have to be extremely careful not to lose control again.

The night after meeting Lillith face to face again, Alex didn't arrive home until after nine. She found Nikki's car in the garage, but she wasn't at home.

Alex called Nikki's cell phone, which went straight to voice mail. This told her one of two things. Either she was on a call with two people or she had it shut off. Alex decided to leave a message in more ways than one. "Where are you?"

As she was leaving the message, her phone beeped.

"Canton," she barked into the phone.

Nikki had tried calling Alex several times. Each time Alex had been on the phone and didn't pick up the second line.

When Alex answered on the third ring, Nikki thought maybe Alex was on the other line with Scott. "Alex, do you need to call me back?"

"No. I just tried calling you but it went right to voice mail, so I left you a message. Where are you and why the fuck is your car here?"

Alex pulled a beer from the refrigerator. Twisting off the cap, she downed half the bottle.

Alex was in a mood and it was only going to deteriorate. Nikki took a deep breath. "When I went to lunch today it started making a weird noise underneath. I decided to bring it home for you to look at when you got home. I didn't want to drive it around and possibly do additional damage."

"What the fuck did you do to it? Did you run over something? How the hell did you get back to work?" Alex felt a pang of fear at the answer.

"The only thing I hit was a pothole. I'm not stupid enough to run over something. You know I'm careful. I don't take any chances when it comes to driving. As for getting back to work, Lillith picked me up from the house."

As soon as it left her mouth, she knew it was a mistake.

Alex saw red before her eyes. Anger caused her to smash the bottle in her hand against the wall. Grinding her teeth together, she tried not to lose control. "Lillith picked you up? Did you give her a tour of the house, stopping in the bedroom last?"

"Alex, stop. Stop those thoughts right there. I changed my clothes before she arrived, then she brought me back to work, that is all." Nikki heard Alex muttering. "Is everything okay there?"

Alex looked down at her bloody hand. "Yeah, just peachy. When are you coming home?" She wrapped a dish towel around her hand.

"That is why I was trying to call you. I am done here for the night. I was calling to see if you were done or would be a while longer. I'll see you in a few, okay?" Nikki knew what the next question would be.

"How are you getting home?" She knew the answer before she asked.

Nikki readied herself for the explosion. "Lillith is bringing me home. Before you go off, don't, because I don't want to hear it. Okay?" She had no idea what possessed her to fight back, but she liked the feeling. Yet at the same time, it terrified her. Fear was her constant companion these days as she pushed it a little more each time. She was fearful that there would come the moment when she pushed Alex just a little too hard, causing her to explode.

"Fine, I'll be waiting." The line disconnected.

Nikki couldn't believe her ears. A shiver ran through her. What had Alex meant by she'd be waiting?

Sometime later Lillith turned her Harley into their driveway. Nikki knew they'd find Alex there waiting for them. What happened next she never expected. Alex walked up, shook Lillith's hand in greeting, thanking her for looking out for Nikki.

Nikki was shocked speechless. This reaction terrified her more than the screaming did. She went with the flow for the moment, fully expecting the anger to show its ugly head as soon as Lillith pulled away.

One thought and one only crossed Alex's mind when she saw the motorcycle pull into the driveway. She was royally screwed. She was now convinced that Lillith was keeping a close eye on Nikki as well as Alex herself.

"If you two will excuse me, I'm going into the house." Nikki made a quick getaway.

Alex decided to play nice with Lillith after Nikki excused herself.

They stood debating the differences between the old style of bikes and the new. It was as Alex leaned against the side of the garage that she noticed an occupied unfamiliar car sitting across the street. Alex had a feeling they were being watched.

Lillith had noticed the car as soon as she pulled onto the street. It was the same car she'd seen several times sitting in the lot next to where Nikki worked. The car gave her an uneasy feeling. She felt rather than saw Alex tense when she laid eyes on the same vehicle.

Lillith questioned Alex on it. "You?"

Alex knew exactly what she was referring to. Lillith was wondering if the person was one of her detectives "No. You?"

Lillith's eyes never left the license plate. She could only make out the first two letters. "Nope."

She blew Alex away when she asked, "When was the last time you heard from the stalker?"

Somehow, Alex knew Nikki would have told her about that. Having it brought out into the open though momentarily shocked her. Alex tried to hide her shock. "It's been a while. I got a feeling though. You?"

Lillith reached behind her under her leather jacket to retrieve her gun. She brought it around, releasing the safety. Alex looked at her with amusement. It was funny how life took sudden turns.

Lillith never took her eyes off her objective. "Yeah."

With that, they both took off at full blast across the street. Momentarily stunned, the person was almost too late in starting the car and taking off before the two women were upon them.

When they heard the engine start, both women put their bodies in overdrive. It was too late though as the car sped off and left them in the dust.

They stood watching it speed away. The two looked at one another, grunted, and walked toward the house. Lillith started her bike and sped away. Alex went into the house, locking the door behind her. She found Nikki in the kitchen pouring a glass of wine.

Nikki knew she shouldn't ask, but couldn't help herself. "Did the two of you have an interesting chat?" She tried not to sound sarcastic, but failed.

Alex walked to her. Pulling her close, she wrapped her arms around Nikki. "Just remember who owns you and we won't have a problem." Alex roughly kissed her. Her lips trailing to Nikki's shoulder, Alex bit her. She bit hard enough to leave a visible marking.

Alex felt Nikki flinch as she bit into her.

"I know who I belong to, how could I ever forget it?" Nikki sighed.

Alex pushed up her shirt. She bit down on her left nipple then sucked on it hard. She heard Nikki gasp trying to pull in deep breaths.

"Are you thinking about her doing this to you?"

After several long heartbeats, her hand made its way inside Nikki's lounge pants through the wetness to their goal. She slipped her fingers inside Nikki, pushing deep.

"Or this?"

Nikki couldn't help what she felt. Even though she wanted to be angry, she couldn't, not when Alex had her hand inside her as she did now. She slowly pulled out and plunged back in hard. Nikki's hips thrust up to meet her hand.

"Do you wish it was her fucking you?" Alex thrust into her again.

"No Alex, only you. Only ever you.... Please...more..."

Alex sucked on her nipple again.

She let Alex take her not because she had no choice, but because that was what she wanted. It had been what felt like an eternity since she had wished for Alex to take control. Most of the time when Alex did, it was not making love, it was not sex. It was just plain fucking. There was no thought in it and it was as far from love as one could get.

The realization hit her that Alex was no longer being overly aggressive. Nikki came as Alex's fingers once more plunged into her. Alex pulled her hand out. Slowly she licked off each of her fingers as Nikki watched. They both knew it was going to be a long night.

†

Arriving at their mini-vacation hotel on Seneca Lake. Alex opened the bottle of wine as Nikki stepped into the bedroom to change.

They visited two of wineries on the way to where they were staying, stopping for lunch along the way at one of the smaller ones. By three in the afternoon, they had checked in at the hotel. They were surprised at being given an upgrade to the honeymoon suite.

Alex finished pouring the wine as Nikki stepped back into the room. Her eyes just about popped from her head. Gulping down the contents of the glass she was holding, she poured another, gulping that down as well.

"Fuck."

Nikki raised her hand, pointed to Alex curling her finger in a come here motion. Alex's brain completely shut down. All coherent thoughts left through her ears as she walked across the room. Nikki stood before her in a black leather corset, laced up the front. It pulled her breasts together pushing them up, making them look twice as big as they were. Alex was positively drooling. She then looked down.

Alex lost her breath altogether. Nothing hid the bulge in the black leather pants Nikki had on. She hadn't even tried. Alex could not even remotely comprehend what Nikki had planned.

Nikki strutted up to her. Taking the glass from Alex's hand, she poured more wine then slowly sipped it. Closing her eyes, Nikki licked her lips. "Mmm… My favorite...."

Setting the glass down, Nikki pulled Alex close, kissing her. "Dance with me." It was not a request. It was a demand.

Sometime later, after the second bottle was empty, Alex was wound tight. Nikki pulled her into the bedroom. There Alex found the covers pulled back, the bed begging to be used. She had no idea what Nikki had planned and she didn't care. She just wanted her, all of her.

Tonight, however, she was soon going to find the roles were to be reversed.

"Strip off your clothes, sit on the edge of the bed and do not move a muscle," Nikki ordered.

Once there Alex watched as Nikki slowly untied the laces. She tried once and only once to reach out and help her.

Nikki smacked her hand away. "No. You are not to touch. If you are a bad girl once more I'll stop and you get to go take a cold shower."

Alex sat rigid and did not bat an eyelash. Her excitement grew at not being able to touch her lover.

She watched as the leather corset fell to the floor. When her eyes landed on Nikki's breasts again, she couldn't believe what she saw. Nikki's left nipple was pierced. Also between her breasts was tattooed a small dagger. It was similar to the large sword on Alex's back, yet unique in its own way. The handle of the dagger curved into the head of panther.

Alex opened her mouth to say something, but no words would come to her. She just simply stared and salivated. When had Nikki gotten those done? She so desperately wanted to lick the valley between those delicious breasts. Alex watched as Nikki's nipples grew hard under her salivating eyes.

Nikki knew exactly where Alex's eyes were glued. "You like? I had them done two weeks ago. Since both of us have been working such long and opposite hours, I was able to keep them a surprise for you." She watched as Alex leered at her. Nikki felt as if her lover wanted to devour her whole.

Nikki slowly pulled the zipper down on the pants. She stopped with it halfway down. "Do you want what I have under here?"

All Alex could do was nod, her eyes never leaving the zipper. Speech left her completely, as well as all rational thought.

Nikki smiled. "Good. Crawl up on the bed, get on your knees and loop your hands through the headboard."

When Nikki had walked into the bedroom earlier she couldn't believe her luck when she saw the brass headboard on the king size bed. Ideas of all kinds flooded into her mind on how she could put it to use. Then she remembered that she had put Alex's handcuffs into her bag.

She watched as Alex put her hands through the spindles on the headboard. Alex then grasped her hands together tightly. She felt the bed move as Nikki climbed onto it. She could feel Nikki on her knees behind her.

Alex felt the zipper of Nikki's leather pants brush up against her bare ass. She groaned at the sensation it caused. Nikki leaned into her harder. Alex in turn groaned louder when she felt the bulge under it. "Do you like that?"

"Yes." Alex was reduced to one-word sentences.

"Good. Close your eyes tightly."

Before Alex knew what was happening, it was already done. Nikki had hidden them under the pillow. In one fluid motion, she pulled out the handcuffs, swiftly attaching them to Alex's hands.

Fear and anger rushed into her. "What the fuck? What are you doing?" Alex pulled against the cuffs, trying to dislodge them.

Reaching around to Alex's chest, Nikki pulled her nipple ring. "Uh, uh." Nikki pinched Alex's nipples so hard it made her twitch. "We're going to play. Except one difference, I'm the one who's going to be in control. Or do you want that cold shower? Hmm?"

She pinched extremely hard again, brushing up against Alex's ass once more. Alex was excited yet angry at the same time. Now that she was handcuffed, she felt a total loss of being able to control the situation. She never had, nor would she ever give herself like this, whether in her personal life or work. Alex hated not being in control, it completely threw her.

Nikki's voice purred huskily into her ear once again. "Well? Fucked or cold shower?"

Alex was too far gone to say no. So instead of fighting it, she went with it, deciding to see how far Nikki would take it. "No… No cold shower. It just threw me for a minute."

Nikki stood on the bed. Steadying herself against the headboard, she resumed stripping out of the pants. "Watch me. Don't take your eyes off me." Alex watched as she peeled the pants down her hips, exposing the harness and dildo.

Alex's breathing became more ragged as the seconds went on. Tonight was all about control.

Nikki was in control of Alex and there was nothing she could do about it. She stepped up to where Alex's head was. She stood, legs spread apart slightly. Alex turned her head to face Nikki. The dildo hung in front of her face perfectly.

"Suck it, get it nice and wet, then maybe I'll use it on you. That is if you're a good girl."

Alex did just as commanded. She pulled it deep into her throat with a powerful sucking motion. Nikki talking to her in this manner excited her further.

Alex sucked on it long and hard. All the while, she was getting more and more excited. Nikki knew that scent, it was Alex's arousal. "Stop.... You're being such a good girl. I guess I'll give you a treat." She moved away from Alex.

"Stick your ass in the air and assume the position." Behind her Nikki slid just under her so that the dildo was positioned under Alex's opening. Before they continued, she made sure the bath towel was under both of them.

Nikki watched as Alex's wetness ran down the inside of her thighs. "Grasp the headboard and lower yourself."

Alex did as commanded, feeling herself being penetrated. "Ah God, Nik… That feels so good." She pulled herself back up. As she did, it slipped out of her.

Nikki reached up grasping Alex's nipple ring between her fingers. She pulled on it. Alex hissed with pleasure, "Yes!"

Nikki could feel the sweet pressure every time Alex lowered herself. "Go slow, go really slow. Whatever you do, don't come, until I tell you to. Understand?!" Nikki placed her hands on Alex's hips and held onto her as Alex once again slowly pulled away from her.

"Yes, yes…feels so good." Alex lowered her body again.

When Nikki could feel the muscles in Alex's thighs begin to tremble, she knew Alex was close to oblivion. It wouldn't be much longer until she couldn't hold the orgasm back, especially when Nikki was having trouble controlling her own from exploding.

She reached behind her under the bed linens to retrieve the items she had hidden there earlier. Nikki first put the latex glove onto her right hand. Then she set the condom-covered dildo beside her. Opening the bottle of lube, she poured a generous amount onto it. She then poured more into the palm of the glove-covered hand.

"Stay where you are, with it inside you. Lean forward, resting your head on your arms. You ready for your special treat?" She caressed Alex's ass with her bare hand.

"Yes, please." Alex groaned. She was begging.

"Well, since you groaned so nicely, how about this?" She then slid two of her lube-covered fingers into Alex's ass. She then pulled out and pushed back in several times, adding another finger as she went. "I know how much you like this. Now, slide up and down again."

Alex did as commanded. She was about to explode. "Nik, can't…much longer…God, it feels too good."

"Ah-ah…not yet. Not quite yet." She then slid her fourth finger in. "I know how much you can take, just like I know how much your ass can take before you explode and scream like a banshee."

Nikki didn't even give Alex a chance to comprehend what she had just said when she felt Nikki's hand leave her and the dildo replace it.

Alex knew she was lost. She came, one orgasm after another ripping through her. She couldn't stop it from happening. She didn't want to stop it. She screamed and screamed as she never had before.

Never before had Alex felt such pleasure. Never before had she wanted Nikki to have her powerless, taking her as she was doing right then and all night long.

Nikki pulled out of Alex, plunging back in hard and deep as Alex slammed herself down upon the harnessed dildo.

"*Yes!*…Oh, God…Nik Yes…fuck me baby…"

Nikki came just as the second wave hit Alex. They both screamed in unison. When Alex pulled up off the dildo Nikki could feel her gushing onto her legs. More continued to run from her as she came repeatedly.

After releasing Alex from her restraints, she pounced on Nikki, their lovemaking continuing until neither could move.

†

A light rapping on the door announced their dinner had arrived. Alex awoke starving.

Throwing on a robe, she opened the door to let the waiter push the cart into the room. After pulling the small table in from the balcony, he arranged several dishes on the table. Outside it had already turned dark, so the small light sconce on the balcony created only a glow, adding to the romance. She tipped him generously as he left. Before waking Nikki, Alex made sure the box was in the pocket of her robe. She sat on the edge of the bed, brushing the hair out of Nikki's eyes. Their lovemaking earlier had blown Alex away.

Nikki had never been like that before. Alex still wasn't sure if she liked it or not. Sure the sex part of it was great, but her being dominated? If Nikki tried to do it again, Alex didn't know if she could go through with it. Possibly, if she didn't know what was coming, like she hadn't today.

Alex wondered from where Nikki had found the sudden inner strength. Never before had she known Nikki to possess such courage. She decided to not dwell on it, she just wanted to enjoy this week, to bring Nikki a little happiness.

I've treated Nikki badly so many times. She's had every right to leave me. Why hasn't she left me, especially after I threatened her? What happened? When did I get so mean?

Alex could feel it in her heart. It happened when she was shot. That split second in time had changed her. Never had she felt so helpless, vulnerable, and something she considered far worse. She had felt afraid. Alex was unable to shake that feeling. That fear had become her constant companion. It never left her. As it built inside her during the months, then years, it had turned into anger. Then it flowered into hatred.

Some days Alex hated everyone and everything surrounding her. Other days, she felt only self-loathing. Those were the mornings when she needed to apologize to Nikki for something, whether it was the ripped clothes, the broken dishes, or the bruises.

Alex knew the feeling for what it was—her mortality. The weakness ate at her insides.

Nikki stirring next to her brought her back to the present. She leaned to brush her lips gently over Nikki's cheek. "Baby, it's time to wake up. I have a little surprise for you."

Sitting up, Nikki pulled the covers up to fight off the chill in the room. She groaned, feeling her back popping back into place. "What time is it, babe?"

Alex brushed her lips across Nikki's. "It's a little after nine. Dinner is served, my lady." She stood holding Nikki's robe open for her.

Nikki sat at the table as Alex pulled the covers from the dishes. After opening the wine, she took her seat across from Nikki.

After finishing the main course, Alex pushed back from the table. "It's nice they can pull this little table inside the room during cold weather. If you put dessert in front of the fireplace, I'll start the fire."

Nikki poured more wine into both glasses as Alex sat next to her.

Pulling the box from her robe, Alex got down on her knees in front of Nikki. Holding the box out, she said, "I'd like for us to get married. That is, if you would like to."

Taking the ring out, she waited.

†

It was the most exquisite piece Nikki had ever seen. It was a wide band made from platinum, yellow and red gold all swirled together. Alex looked up, their eyes meeting. Nikki suddenly found herself speechless. She could only nod as the tears ran down her face.

Alex slipped the ring on her finger beside the one already there. "What date would you like to pick, my love?" She sat on the sofa, taking Nikki into her arms.

"I love you Alex. How about the end of March? Does that sound good?"

"Anything you want, love, anything at all."

Nikki slid from the sofa onto her knees in front of Alex. Parting the robe her lover wore, Nikki lowered her head. "I love you…so very much."

Alex felt her breath upon her bare skin, then her tongue. "Yes!" It was going to be a very long night.

†

Scott looked across the car once more at his friend, after picking her up at the bar. That was what she was tonight, his friend, not co-worker. He was dumbfounded. Scott still couldn't believe what Alex had told him.

"You're actually going to go through with it? The whole thing, even the 'death do us part thing' and the 'monogamy' thing. You do know that means no cheating.... Alex, are you sure you can do this?"

"Jesus, you and Kir have no faith in me. She said the same thing. Scott, I love her and I want to make her happy. I've been such a fuckin' shit for so long. I want to make it up to her." Alex looked out the window. The scenery flew by them, making her nauseous.

"Do you hear yourself, Alex? You asked her because you wanted to make it up to her for your being such an asshole. That's no reason for getting married. Shit, Alex, don't do this to her if that is the reason for it. She'll eventually figure it out. Probably the very first time she catches you cheating on her again after the wedding."

Alex whipped her head around and glared at him.

"Oh, come on, Alex. You really don't think she doesn't know. She only doesn't say anything because she loves you so much. Plus she still thinks you'll change." He put on the turn signal, merging over to exit the expressway.

"Has she said somethin' to you?" Alex pulled her cell phone from her belt after fighting a few moments with the case it was in. Her finger coordination seemed to have left her.

"No, and she doesn't need to. I can see it in her eyes when she looks at you. Especially when I bring you home, like tonight."

He could hear the abhorrence in his own voice. Their wedding was around the corner and here she was drunk and screwing around.

She closed the cell phone without dialing. Alex knew he was right. She'd stepped over the line that evening once again. Alex had stopped off at one of her old hangouts to play some pool before heading home and found herself having one too many drinks. The next thing she knew her hands were down another woman's pants. She ended up calling Scott to take her home when the bartender, an old friend of hers, threatened to call Nikki.

She slumped against the car door. "I fucked up yet again, didn't I?"

"I don't think I even need to answer that. You already answered it yourself. You're the one who has to look yourself in the mirror in the morning and live with yourself. You need to straighten your shit out,

Alex, before it's too late. I really don't know why she puts up with you." He sighed, pulling into her driveway.

Scott thought to himself that some days he didn't know how he put up with her either. He just hoped to hell Nikki was not still awake.

The front door opened as Scott practically carried her up the steps.

Scott mumbled under his breath. "Not good, not good at all. It's only six days until the wedding."

Alex knew she'd been retreating back into her old self again. She couldn't help if the women found her. She never went looking for them. Sure, she was someplace she really shouldn't have been, especially when she told Nikki she'd be home hours ago for dinner, but she had only gone there to play pool. Now here she was, smelling of sex, cigarettes and so drunk Scott had to help her up the steps.

Nikki's heart broke a little more at the condition Alex was in. With a little less than a week until the wedding it seemed things were steadily going downhill. "Put her in the spare room. She can sleep it off in there."

As Scott was leaving, Nikki thanked him once more for bringing her home. After checking on the passed out Alex again, she went to their bedroom. Nikki crawled between the covers once more, alone. She knew sleep would be some time in coming that night.

Lying awake, Nikki watched the moonlight dance across the ceiling. She to be up early too. She wished she could put off the meeting, but she didn't have a choice. Then there was the video conference. Damn, damn, damn…she was so not in the mood to see her face on the screen. Rolling over, Nikki cried herself to sleep once more.

†

Stalking out of the conference room, Nikki slammed the door behind her. She just couldn't believe the arrogance of that woman. "I can't believe she actually sent one of her flunkies, in her place, for the yearly board meeting. The arrogance of her…!"

Anger radiated from every pore as the elevator descended to the lobby. She exited without thinking about where she was headed. Lillith was behind the desk as always. Lately Nikki found herself appraising the woman.

Lillith was strong, but not in just the physical sense. Everything about the woman was intense. Nikki wished on several occasions that she had met her long ago. The way Lillith treated her made her feel special, wanted.

Nikki had long conversations with Lillith, about everything in the universe. Never once though did she make her feel inferior. She treated Nikki like an intelligent and funny woman. Lillith never talked down to her as if she were just an object.

"Lillith, I need to get out of here. It's late in the day, let's go get a drink." Nikki leaned against the desk, waiting for Lillith to decide.

Lillith knew something was wrong that morning when Nikki blew by her, not bothering to

193

say good morning. That had been an immediate tip-off. The only time Nikki didn't stop to say hello was when she and Alex had a bad night or weekend.

Now she looked outraged, ready to decapitate someone. Watching out for Nikki had become more than just a job to her. Lillith had unexpectedly come to care about Nikki. It had now become her own personal quest to keep Nikki safe and happy, no matter what the cost.

"Sure, I was just shutting down the computer and getting ready to lock up for the evening. As soon as I am finished we can go."

They walked the several blocks to the bar and grill that they had lunch at almost every day. As they walked, Lillith scanned the area surrounding them for any threat. The habit had become second nature decades ago.

A second person brushed up against Nikki on the crowded street. Lillith moved closer, slipping her right hand onto the small of her companion's back.

It felt so natural for Lillith's hand to be where it was. Nikki felt the warmth spread through her. Tilting her head slightly, she looked up at the much taller woman. Smiling at Lillith, she silently thanked her for the protection.

Lillith motioned to the server for a second round of beers, when the first one lasted only a matter of minutes. Nikki looked down at the empty beer bottle, realizing she had picked half the label off. Looking across the table, she wondered once again how this woman was able to draw things out of her just by her presence alone.

"And you never judge me..." Nikki said quietly, not realizing Lillith would hear her in the crowded bar.

"Never."

"God, I needed that. Sorry I seem like such a bitch today. It was a bad night last night, or should I say early this morning. Then this shit today. I so didn't need it." She quieted her thoughts as the waitress set the fresh beers down, taking the empties away. Once again, she appraised Lillith.

"I'm sorry, I...I...it just seems lately you're always here when I need you. Sometimes I feel like I'm always dumping on you." Nikki sighed. "I'm ashamed I ever let it get this bad. Before you suggest any such thing, no, I will never go to the police." She held up her hand. "I know you're my friend yet so much more. Never in my life have I had someone I felt I could tell *anything* to. You're quite obviously physically strong enough to handle anyone or anything. The first time we talked about Alex, I was terrified you were going to find her and kill her. No matter what, you never flew off the handle, you're always so calm. It's kind of disconcerting actually." Nikki became silent as she thought about the woman sitting across from her.

"Nikki, you are my friend. I would never do anything to hurt you. There are things in a person's life that only they can work out. Yes, I could take care of it, but in the end, you would hate me for it. This is something you must do yourself. Whether you realize it or not you are a strong woman. I'm talking about your spirit. You are capable of far more than you realize. I take it something happened with Alex last night?"

When Nikki sniffled, Lillith picked up her beer instead of reaching across the table. She fought every urge of her body not to scoop this woman up and whisk her away to her house in Londonderry, Ireland. "Before you continue…have you ever been to Ireland?"

"No. I've always wanted to go though."

"Maybe someday you will."

"Lillith, you've never told me anything about your family. Do you have brothers or sisters? Are your parents still alive?"

A rare show of emotion showed on Lillith's face. "I have no family left."

So few words about her family intrigued Nikki. "Do they live elsewhere and you never get to see them?" Nikki was pushing.

"My family are buried in South Dakota. My older sister was named after the state that my parents loved so much."

This was the first personal information Lillith had shared with Nikki. "Oh, so you have a sister, what line of work is she in?"

"She is with the rest of my family."

Nikki knew then that something horrific must have happened when her friend was young. "Lillith, are all of your family members dead?"

"Yes." Lillith was a woman of few words as always.

"Oh my, I'm sorry. Were you young? Was there some sort of accident?"

Lillith's head bowed. "It made me into what I became. I can say no more. Now, please go on…something happened last night that you were going to tell me about."

"You could say that. She called Scott to bring her home early this morning. She couldn't even stand up without help." Nikki studied a spot on the table, unable to look up at Lillith.

Lillith knew there was more. She didn't prod, knowing Nikki would continue when she could. When she still remained silent, Lillith coaxed her just a hair. "And…" She watched as Nikki's tears flowed freely. Lillith was grateful once again that they always sat in a back booth away from the main flow of traffic.

"Alex was drunk and smelled like week old sex. She… oh God, Lillith she terrifies me. One moment she can be so loving and the next I don't know who she is." Nikki faltered. She was ashamed that anyone had to hear this, especially Lillith. "I just don't understand. Things were getting better. Now, with the wedding less than a week away… it's just… I keep thinking she'll change. That she'll be the woman that I fell in love with again. She won't stop though, will she? Not until she kills me. I don't want to leave her. I don't feel I have a choice anymore though. God, Lillith what am I going to do? I feel the only reason she wants us to get married is because that's what I want. It's not what she wants, not really. Please, I need someone to tell me." Nikki felt her inner strength dissolving into the hollowness she felt within.

Lillith finally reached across the table. Taking Nikki's hand in hers was something she never expected herself to do. Startling Nikki, she put her hand to her lips, kissing the palm of it. Lillith needed to quiet the anger rising in heart.

"No one can tell you what to do. You have to find your own path. Only you can know your own mind and heart. Please think hard and long before doing anything, including marrying her. You need to look inside yourself to know if it's the right thing to do. Yes, I have come to care deeply for you, we are friends, but I cannot make this decision for you. You must above all else, keep yourself safe. Something else happened today, this afternoon, didn't it?" Lillith squeezed her hands.

"You read me so well. I don't deserve someone like you in my life." She smiled up at Lillith.

"No, you deserve better, but I will try to be the best friend that I know how."

Nikki stared into her eyes then once again lowered them to the table. "Lillith, I…thank you. You mean so much to me." She left what had just happened between them for later discussion.

"My morning seemed to have gone from bad to worse. I received a call from Alex informing me that it was Ann who was sitting outside our house the other day that she and you saw. She confessed to Alex that she had been checking up on me as she calls it. I call it stalking. I wouldn't doubt it if she still is. She denies though that she's the one sending us the horrible items. Then I had a video board meeting.

The woman who runs the other office is an old friend of mine. Well, I thought she was a friend. Anyway, instead of her attending the meeting she sent one of her lackeys. He didn't even have an answer when questioned as to why she wasn't there. Only that she had called him and told him to attend the meeting because she couldn't. She just didn't have the balls to show her face to me."

Feeling the anger rolling off Nikki, Lillith knew exactly who she was referring to. She needed to defuse the situation. She wished Rory would return to Nikki, tell her everything, then take her as far away from Alex as possible. Lillith could spirit Nikki away, take her to Rory, forcing her to come clean. Lillith wouldn't though. She'd promised Rory not to interfere when they spoke earlier that morning.

Lillith found herself caring for Nikki. She, however, would not act upon those feelings out of respect and honor to Rory. Her honor to Rory was the least of what stopped her. Nikki deserving so much better than what she can ever give her stopped Lillith mid-thought.

In many ways, she was no better than Alex. In others, she was far worse than the destructive detective ever dared to dream of being. In the farthest reaches of her heart, Lillith felt she was nowhere near deserving of a woman as wonderful as Nikki.

Lillith felt Nikki was having doubts about staying with Alex. She knew Nikki had already started to stand up for herself against Alex. Lillith couldn't help but step in. To give Nikki just a little nudge. What could it hurt?

"Nikki, I would like for you to listen to me. To listen clearly to what I am saying. Always remember that every single human being does the things they do for a reason. You are a good and wonderful person. Any woman would be honored to have you love them. Maybe this woman knows that. Could it be she felt remorse and guilt for what she did? Possibly, she could not face you out of this guilt. It does no good to dwell on the rest. It will only eat at you from the inside. It is not healthy. You are cared about, Nikki, very much so. That is why you must do what is in your heart in regard to Alex, not what you think is the right thing to do. Others will help. All you need to do is to ask. Do you understand me?"

Nikki smiled. She felt loved more in the past few moments, than in all the rest of her life.

"Yes. Completely...."

As they sat, they drank several more beers, talking about the little things in life. Nikki kept coming back to two things. Could she continue on the way things were going? Could she marry Alex?

Nikki came to one conclusion. No, she could not. Both Rory and Lillith had showed her she deserved better. It had just taken her longer than most to see it. For the first time she saw everything clearly.

"I love Alex, but that's no longer enough." Nikki stood next to the booth.

"I have to go, Lil'. I'll see you in the morning. I'm going home. It's time Alex and I have a very serious talk. At the very least, there can be no wedding. As for leaving her...I just don't see us together any longer. I want out of this relationship one way or another. Thank you for everything. I feel like I've stepped out of the fog. It's like I can breathe again."

Leaning over, she gently kissed Lillith on the lips. "Thank you, so very much."

Nikki didn't stop for a moment to contemplate her next words. They came from the heart. "Tell me, oh wise, tall one, does someone like say…" Nikki hesitated a moment. "…say like myself, interest someone, let us say, like yourself?" She feared either answer.

Lillith sat frozen momentarily, then was beside Nikki in less than a heartbeat. Had Lillith heard the words correctly? Could Nikki be asking what Lillith thought she was? No, Lillith could never allow it.

It always amazed Nikki how fast Lillith could move and how silently.

Lillith steeled her heart, speaking some of the toughest words she would ever have to. "Someone like me should not be and never will be of any interest to anyone. That is the only way it can be." She dropped her gaze to her black leather cowboy boots, observing that they needed a good polishing.

Nikki heard what she was saying along with what she wasn't. Nikki drew Lillith's attention back to her. Squeezing the much larger hand, Nikki looked into eyes that reflected only coldness back at her. She shivered, suddenly feeling chilly.

"That is where you are incorrect. You are a champion who deserves only the best. Do not doubt that for one moment. Never dispute that you deserve true happiness with someone who is your equal standing beside you, yet worships the ground you walk on."

The enormous woman standing next to her felt she wasn't deserving of a life, which saddened Nikki more than anything had before. Lillith had treated her with nothing but respect and honor. Therefore, she couldn't contemplate her being anything else but a kind and gentle creature.

Nikki smiled. "Yes, you deserve everything."

"I will be at home, if you have need of me. If you find you need someplace to go after talking with Alex, please consider my home a safe haven." Lillith held the door of the pub open for Nikki. She thought of the words exchanged between them. She remained unmoved in her convictions.

"I deserve nothing," she muttered quietly, thinking her companion couldn't hear her.

Nikki walked a little ahead, with her back to the quiet woman. Nikki smiled again. She had heard what was she wasn't meant to. What were meant to be but a mere whisper on the wind, were words uttered in response. "You deserve the world my love, the world."

Lillith's heart warmed slightly.

†

When Nikki and Lillith had first arrived at the pub they had been so wrapped up in what they had been discussing, neither noticed the woman seated moments after their arrival. Additionally neither saw a woman, with ice-cold eyes, dressed in leather astride her motorcycle watching them as they had entered the bar.

Motorcycle woman watched through the window as the larger woman kissed Nikki's hand, shortly after arriving. She drove away feeling insanity boiling its way to the surface.

No one really knows what makes a person turn. Studies can be done, books written on the irrational or even psychopathic behavior of an individual. In the end there is only one person who truly knows the reason behind their world closing in on them. All of the whys or hows asked may never be answered. For sometimes there is no answer, only more questions.

There comes a moment in time when all life comes full circle. Where you are… what you do with it depends on many factors. If your soul is strong enough, you can take your own destiny by the horns and shape it as you desire. If you are not, it will destroy you without remorse, without regret or honor.

✝

Tipsy from the beer, Nikki carefully pulled into the garage. She noticed Alex's motorcycle had been moved from where it had been that morning. Closing the garage door, Nikki entered the house. After setting her laptop and briefcase on the kitchen table, Nikki continued to the living room and stopped suddenly.

On the floor lay her wedding dress, torn to shreds. Littered around the room were empty beer bottles. Bending over, Nikki picked up a piece of the dress. "Who would do such a thing? Why?"

The beer in her threatened to come up as she called out. "Alex?"

The house was eerily quiet. Nikki knew Alex must be home. Her truck and motorcycle both were in the garage. Her personal effects, which Alex would never go anywhere without, were on the table.

Nikki turned to look at the CD player. The first thing Alex did every night was turn on her music, making sure it was loud. Something was very wrong.

"Where are you?"

Grabbing the phone, Nikki called the only person she knew could help.

✝

When the phone rang, Lillith saw Nikki's name on the caller ID. Nikki had told her that she was going home to tell Alex she was calling off the wedding and possibly leave her. Knowing Alex's temper Lillith became concerned. "Nikki, is everything okay?"

"Lil', I'm home. Something is wrong. Please hurry."

Lillith pulled to the curb. "Is it Alex?"

Nikki looked around the room. "Yes, it's too quiet here…all the lights are out and her keys are still on the table."

"Is her truck and motorcycle there?" Lillith's concern grew.

"Yes. This isn't like her. You know how regimented she is."

Lillith made a U-turn. Speeding toward Nikki's home, she wished Nikki would listen to her. "I'm only a couple of miles away. Go back outside and wait for me."

"I can't, Lil. Maybe she's fallen or something…maybe in the shower. I need to make sure she's all right."

Lillith pounded her fist on the steering wheel. "Don't! I'm almost there. Just go outside and wait. Please."

Something hit the floor above Nikki. "I'm sorry, Lil. She might need help. Just hurry."

"Nikki?" Lillith heard only silence on the phone. Nikki had hung up. "Damn!"

†

Standing at the bottom of the stairs Nikki was afraid to go up them but was worried that Alex might need her. She had to go. Slowly, silently, she ascended the steps. Her hands shook badly, causing her to grip the railing tightly in one hand and the phone tighter in the other.

Heart pounding she paused on the top step to listen and heard crying coming from one of the bedrooms. She could hear muttering from inside the room. Slowly Nikki opened the door.

The room was a disaster. Beer bottles littered the floor. Bed sheets were shredded and scattered everywhere. In the middle of the debris sat Alex. Nikki had never felt more terrified in her life. Tentatively stepping over the mess, she slowly made her way to Alex.

†

Alex looked up from the knife that she held in her hand. She looked at the woman who stood before her, the woman who had betrayed her. "Why?"

She crouched in front of Alex. She was terrified but she had to try. "Alex, what's going on sweetie? What's wrong? What happened here?"

Standing, Alex pulled Nikki to her and set the knife on the bedside table. The rage was clear on Alex's face, just as the terror was on Nikki's. Alex had her hand wrapped around her arm. It was so tight she couldn't shake it off.

"Alex, please you're scaring me. What's going on?"

"What's going on? Why don't you tell me?"

Alex slapped her across the face. "Hmm? Are you letting her fuck you?" She hit her again, harder.

"Please Alex, no…there's only you…only you. Please, I love you. Please stop this, you're hurting me." Nikki tried to get away from her once more.

Alex grabbed her by her hair, pulling her head back to expose her neck. She sank her teeth into her, drawing blood. "You're mine. You belong to me.

You're my property. You will always belong to me, even in death. Then no one else can touch you." She slammed Nikki's head on the wall and let go of her.

Nikki slid down the wall onto the floor. The room before her blurred and spun. She couldn't stop the sobs that started. "Alex, please stop. This isn't you. You're better than this. You can be a good person. I love you, please."

Alex grabbed Nikki once more by the hair, pulling her across the room. What Alex had not seen Nikki do with her hand would end it all, but would there be anything left to find? Anything… anyone living…

Alex ripped Nikki's clothes off then threw her onto the bed. "What do you think about when she's fucking you? Are you thinking about me? About our life together? Our marriage? How could you do this to me?" She grabbed Nikki's nipples and twisted painfully. Nikki screamed.

"Alex, stop it right now! I've never cheated on you, never. You have to stop this. I have only ever loved you." Nikki was begging Alex with all her heart. She tried crawling across the bed to reach the knife.

Alex grabbed Nikki by the ankle. She pulled her from the bed, throwing her against the other night table. She landed on the table, crying out in pain as she hit her lower back hard on the corner.

"I saw you. I saw the two of you together. I saw her kiss you. You're a whore! You were fucking Rory too, weren't you?" Alex punched her in the face.

Pulling Nikki from the floor, Alex threw her onto the bare mattress. As she held her to the bed with her body, she slammed her fingers into Nikki's body. First two, then three penetrated her. Through the brutal assault Alex screamed, "Mine! Mine! Mine!"

Something inside of Nikki finally snapped. After all the other beatings, they had always made up and then went on with life. There would be no making up this time. She wanted an end to it. She could take no more.

Getting her feet under Alex, Nikki pushed her away. "No! No more. I have never cheated on you. You're the one who slept around. I have only ever loved you, making excuse after excuse for you. Now that won't even be enough to save it. How can you say you love me? How can you honestly say that, when you treat me like this?"

The years of anger welled up inside of Nikki, causing her to fight back. Nikki slapped at her, scratched, and even tried biting her to get free. Unfortunately, Alex was much stronger than her to begin with. Couple that with the insanity and alcohol burning within her, it made Alex's strength double what it was naturally.

Alex picked her up, pinning her against the wall with a hand around her neck. "No, the only thing I can honestly say now is that you're an ugly, fat, filthy whore. No wonder I went looking elsewhere for sex. You deserve what you're going to get."

She watched as the blood trailed its way down Nikki's face from the cut on her forehead, from hitting the wall.

✝

For a split moment, Alex's eyes softened. Then it was gone, replaced once more with emptiness. Nikki looked into Alex's eyes. This wasn't Alex. All she saw before her was an animal…a scared and cornered animal. Her eyes went wide as she saw Lillith in the doorway.

✝

Alex saw the look on Nikki's face.

As Alex turned toward the door, she pulled the gun from her waistband that Nikki hadn't noticed before. By the time Nikki screamed, the gun had been fired and the bullet found its home. She watched as Lillith dropped to the floor.

Alex smiled. "Ha!" she yelled triumphantly. "Thought one bullet couldn't take you down, bitch?"

Nikki prayed to whatever God was listening, that her second SOS had gotten out.

It had indeed gotten out. As he entered through the wide open front door, he heard the gunshot. Sprinting up the steps, his gun was already drawn. Scott stopped in his tracks when he saw Lillith lying in the doorway to the bedroom. Pulling her into the hallway, he checked for a pulse. She was still breathing, but barely. He grabbed a piece of what looked like torn bed linen and pressed it against Lillith's neck. Knowing it probably wouldn't do much good, but he did it anyway, he moved her hand so it was pressed against the temporary bandage. Slowly he edged his way into the room.

The sight before him made him want to retch. He held the bile down as he took in the situation. The woman holding Nikki once more off the floor against the wall was not his partner, not his best friend in the world. She was a murderer. Nikki was naked and covered in blood, her head hanging forward. He couldn't tell if she was alive. Scott thought for sure she was dead. No one could have survived this brutality.

Alex held Nikki with one hand while the other held the gun to Nikki's temple. Before it ended, Alex had to confess her last sin. A sin that she knew would blow Nikki's mind. She stroked the side of Nikki's face with the gun.

"Oh, my sweet innocent Nikki, you really don't know, do you? I couldn't help myself. When I was shot....I felt fear for the first time. Fear that I couldn't protect you. Fear that you would find me weak. Fear that you would leave me for someone else. I thought that you would leave me if I showed weakness. I had to make you mine, only mine. I needed to give you something else to fear, to make you need me more than anyone else in the world. I had to make you understand. It didn't work though, did it? Not even hiding your keys and phone stopped you from going to them."

It was then that all became clear to Nikki. Alex had sent the boxes and the letters. She had been the one hiding the objects. Nikki sobbed. "Oh, God…no…."

Scott breathed a small sigh of relief. Nikki was alive for the moment at least.

Nikki and Scott each silently blamed themselves. If only they had been stronger, stood up to Alex sooner…. If they had made her seek help, lives would possibly have turned out so differently. If so, lives might have been spared pain and one might have been spared the ultimate sacrifice.

Nikki knew in her heart Lillith couldn't have survived the gunshot just as Scott knew that she would most likely bleed-out in the hallway.

He heard Nikki's raspy voice. "I gave you everything, Alex. I gave you my heart, my soul, my dignity… My everything… You have taken everything else, so why not take my life? Just do it, Alex." Thinking Lillith dead because of her calling her for help, she added, "I have nothing left now. Just do it. Please."

Scott could take no more. This needed to end. "Alex, drop the gun and let go of Nikki."

Alex had known who was there before he had even spoken. She had known who it was when she heard the bottom step creak. Alex found it ironic that it would be him there in the end. That it would be him that would be the one to end it. She leaned in and kissed Nikki gently on the lips.

Quietly she spoke. Only Nikki could hear Alex's words. "I'm sorry, so sorry. I do love you more than anything else in the world. I love you more than life. I can't help myself any longer and it has to end. There's only one way."

"Alex, please I don't want to shoot you. Drop the gun." He pulled the safety off his gun.

"You know that's not going to happen. You know what you have to do."

He saw the muscle twitch in her arm.

Scott didn't hesitate— he took the shot. He knew Alex was pulling the trigger as he pulled his.

Her gun went off as well, but not until it had changed where it was aimed and the bullet only grazed Nikki.

His bullet found its mark and both women slumped to the floor. Even as hurt as she was, Nikki screamed in pain as she pulled Alex into her arms.

Scott didn't know whether it was from the physical pain or the pain in her heart that Nikki screamed, only that he cried with her as his own heart broke. He watched as she pulled Alex into her arms, trying to soothe her. Knowing there was only one thing to do, Scott called Captain Mahoney, told him he was needed and to send an ambulance, although knowing they'd be too late.

They both knew what Alex had done. She knew of only one way she could stop. She needed someone to stop her. Much later that night Scott would find a missed call and voice mail from Alex. The voice mail contained only two words-*Help me*.

Nikki tried stopping the flow of blood from Alex's neck but knew it was futile. She was bleeding out. She was dying. Now was the time to make peace,

Alex needed to know that she loved her, that there had never been anyone else.

Nikki knew she couldn't let onto Alex that she knew her lover wasn't going to make it. She had to be positive…to be loving.

She pushed the hair back from Alex's face. "Hang on, baby, please, for me. Scott says help is on the way. I love you, Alex. I've always loved you. There's never been anyone else ever other than you. Please love, hang on. You are my heart. You have to hang on. I don't know how to survive without you. You're the strong one. You've always taken care of me. Please, Alex…I need you."

Even with holding her hand over the hole, Alex's life continued to gush forth. She looked up at Scott then bent her head to Alex's. She gently kissed her on the lips, knowing it would probably be for the last time.

✝

As she kissed her Alex's mind raged its final thoughts. She had to tell Nikki, she had to voice the words. With her last remaining strength, she opened her eyes as best she could. Alex saw Michael, God's Archangel standing behind Nikki.

Nikki watched as Alex slowly opened her eyes. She was speechless.

For the first time in her life, Alex spoke only from her heart. "My wife. I'm sorry. My angel…may God forgive me…"

Silence…

At times it is a wondrous thing. At other times it is heart wrenching. At that particular moment, it brought forth only agony as the silence was broken with what could only be described as an animal screaming in pain.

†

Lives had been altered. Souls shattered. Time and existence had changed.

However, one thing remained steadfast throughout it all. What had needed to be done had been done. The beast had been stopped.

Chapter Six

In the End

Kirstin knew what had happened between Alex and Nikki. It comforted Nikki to know that Kirstin did not hate her. Nikki overheard a conversation between Kirstin and Lillith a few days before the funeral.

Lillith signed herself out of the hospital that morning...against doctor's orders. She had the need to visit Nikki that evening. Nikki had been asleep on the couch when she heard voices in the kitchen and recognized her two friends' voices. One was Lillith's and the other Kirstin's.

"I can't blame her one bit for feeling no remorse. I could never have endured what she did. When did things go so wrong? When did Alex change? I blame myself. She was my sister and I knew something was wrong. I just never thought it would come to this." Kirstin shouldered the blame more than she should have.

Lillith tried to reassure Kirstin. "There are no easy answers. None of us is fully to blame. Each of us knew something was amiss but we could not have helped either of them, until they admitted there was a problem. We will help Nikki pick up the pieces and hope she can move on. She is one of the strongest people I have met. She just has not yet come to know it. She will make it. We will make sure of it."

"You're pretty damn smart, Lillith. What did you do before coming here?" Nikki could hear curiosity in Kirstin's voice.

Nikki wanted to hear her reply so she remained in the living room. Lillith's deep laugh drifted down the hall. "I deleted humanity's problems."

"Ooo…kay. And are you still deleting humanity's problems?"

"No, I retired the day I met a certain short, green-eyed spitfire. Who happens to be awake and standing in the living room listening to us."

Having been caught, Nikki froze. Then she heard Kirstin laughing.

"Very funny, Kirstin…ha, ha…" Nikki said as she opened the door.

Lillith puzzled her. Nikki hoped one day to figure her out. Walking into the kitchen, she laughed at the two of them. They sat at the kitchen table drinking from juice boxes and eating cheese sticks that she kept in the refrigerator for when Kirstin brought the kids over. "Hey, those are for the kids, you moochers."

Wrapping Lillith in a hug, Nikki kissed her on the cheek. "You are too freakin' funny, woman. I'd like very much to discuss later how you know things like that."

✝

At the funeral, sitting in the chair reserved for the grieving spouse, she felt out of place. When losing a wife one should be heartsick about the loss. Nikki wondered repeatedly during the past two weeks if maybe there wasn't something wrong with her. It felt liberating the day Alex died. She could start healing. There would be no more beatings, no more guilt.

When had things gone so horribly wrong in her life? How did she end up there? If Nikki had left Alex, would this have turned out differently? All Nikki had wanted was to be loved.

The anger Nikki felt was about what had been taken from her. Alex had stolen her life and Nikki would fight to get it back. That much she had learned from the past five years. No one would ever take advantage of her again. She had gained strength. Nikki now had the backbone she had lacked for most of her life, resulting in everyone using her as a trampoline. Sitting by Alex's casket, Nikki was resolved that no one would ever abuse her again, in any form.

She was free now. However, was she really? The sudden doubt made her nervous. Would Nikki ever be free, or would Alex continue to haunt her? Scanning the crowd, Nikki found several friendly faces. Two were Mark and his wife, the other, Liz.

Mark and Janet's kindness had been beyond words. He was more than a boss. Mark had become a friend, which Nikki was grateful for. His wife Janet showed up on Nikki's porch every evening since Alex's death. Some nights she would arrive with home baked dinners, some with desserts. Cooking was Janet's way of dealing with all that had happened.

Liz stayed close to Nikki in case she was needed. Nikki tried to convince Liz not to blame herself, but she didn't seem to be getting through to her.

Kirstin squeezing Nikki's hand conveyed support. Nikki was sure without it, she would never have made it.

Everything got hectic, taking days to plan the funeral. Cutting through the red tape of burying a police officer was almost impossible. Everyone breathed a sigh of relief when it was through.

Liz was the only friend that remained with Nikki through the years. Sometimes their only contact had been at work. Alex had tried her best to drive Liz away, but she held steadfast, refusing to budge.

Scott sat back further, even though Nikki had asked him to join her in the front. He refused, blaming himself for what had happened. The day of the incident Nikki spent the night in the hospital to be observed for the blow to the head, Scott had broken down as he sat with her. He told her there should've been something he could've done to stop her.

At the time Scott still had hope that Alex was going to turn her life around: that was until moments before her death when she begged Nikki for forgiveness. Scott sat through that night with Nikki. Seeing him so depressed, her heart hurt for him.

Forgiveness. Was that supposed to wash it all away, to make it all better? Nikki couldn't help but chuckle. Looking around she stifled the laugh, not wanting anyone to think she was losing her mind.

†

The minister stood on the other side of the casket as it was lowered. Reading from the open bible, he seemed unaffected by the occasional gust of wind that pelted him with rain. "Ashes to ashes, dust to dust…We lay to rest one of our finest today, Lt. Alexandria Michelle Canton. Taken from us at the early age of thirty-six years, she will be greatly missed by all…."

Perhaps the silence brought Nikki from her reveries. Embarrassed, she realized Reverend LaSalle had been waiting for her to do something. Nikki had missed the end of his sermon.

He waited patiently as Nikki sat there, afraid to move. Thank heavens for Kirstin. She gently took Nikki's arm. "It's time."

She nodded. Nikki knew what she had to do. When Nikki stood, her knees almost buckled under her. Falling on her face would be embarrassing. "I'm okay Kirstin, thank you," she said quietly.

Taking roses from an arrangement beside the casket, Reverend LaSalle handed each of them one as they approached. Each person lay them on the casket as they passed, saying one last good-bye.

Hesitating, Nikki couldn't remember what to do next. Sure, she had dumped a girlfriend before, but she had never buried one. For a moment, she thought she had put voice to her thoughts. Looking around quickly, Nikki found no one staring at her in horror. Was she truly losing her last shred of sanity?

Ahead of Nikki, Kirstin's Aunt Cassandra cornered Kirstin on the way to the limo. Not wishing to deal with the overbearing woman, Nikki didn't stop. Behind her she could hear Kirstin trying to evade the older woman.

Finally rid of Aunt Cassandra Kirstin walked faster, to catch up with Nikki. Kirstin wanted to make sure she wasn't upset. Nikki stopped in her tracks, causing Kirstin almost to knock her down.

"Honey, what's wrong?" Following Nikki's line of sight, she saw a woman standing by a black SUV.

They looked at one another. Puzzled, they spoke in unison. "What the Hell?" Looking back, no one was there.

When Tom finally strolled up to them, Nikki asked him, "Did you see?"

"See what? What's going on?" Confused, Tom looked at Nikki then Kirstin.

"I'll tell you later dear." She felt sorry for him. Half the time he seemed to arrive a minute too late.

Turning to Nikki, Kirstin lied. She didn't want to admit who she thought it was. "Nikki I'm not sure who was there, if anyone. It's been a long day and we're both tired. Let's just get you home, okay?"

"Okay. Guess my eyes were playing tricks. I know she wouldn't have the balls to show up here today." Lowering her head slightly, Nikki tried to hide her weariness. Nikki's eyebrows scrunched together, her mind working overtime.

"Nikki, don't. She's not worth wasting your time on." Kirstin knew Nikki couldn't quite let it go.

Nikki wondered why aloud, "Why would she show up now? She wouldn't have anything to gain by it." Nikki pinched her nose, which told Kirstin she had a migraine coming on.

Putting her arm around Nikki, Kirstin asked, "What are you thinking right this moment?"

Looking off into the distance, Nikki sighed. "There's one person missing on this day. She was there when I needed someone the most. She never stopped coming back."

Maybe Nikki's heart wasn't as dead as she thought it was. That caused Kirstin to smile. She truly hoped Lillith would stick around. And fight for what was in her heart, because Kirstin knew Lillith was in love with Nikki. She could see it in Lillith's eyes the first time she spoke with her.

Kirstin laid her hand on Nikki's shoulder. "It's time to go."

She looked up at Kirstin. "Oh, sorry, I guess I wandered there for a moment."

Once in the limo so many thoughts ran through Kirstin's mind. Some Nikki had answered others she evaded. One of those had to do with Lillith.

Kirstin saw the love in her eyes for Nikki, even though the hardened woman tried valiantly hiding it. Being curious if the feelings were returned

Kirstin asked Nikki. She immediately became flustered, refusing to answer her directly. It was then that Kirstin knew for sure. Nikki loved Lillith.

Kirstin told her that she would never begrudge her being happy. If it was with Lillith, then so be it. In the end, that was all any of them wanted for Nikki. She watched as a tear ran down Nikki's cheek.

Nikki hesitated a second. "I really did love her you know. Even with all that happened. I've never stopped loving her. I hoped the change was permanent when she changed back to the woman I met five years ago. I guess it wasn't meant to be." She begged Kirstin to understand.

"I know sweetie, I know. All of us will be here for you, to help you through this." Shaking her head Kirstin knew it was going to be a very long day.

†

Rory didn't mean for Nikki to see her yet. She wanted to wait until there were fewer people around. During the past few weeks, Rory had thought a lot about what she would say to Nikki. Her resolve not to interfere in their lives almost ended that afternoon in the pub. Rory climbed into her truck still mumbling to herself. "That was the day Alex got what she deserved for hurting Nikki."

Her greatest concern had always been for Nikki's happiness. Rory had finally admitted to herself that she was wrong in leaving. "I should never have left you. I thought I was doing what was right. I thought Alex would change. You and Lil' paid the price for my stupidity."

Turning her key in the ignition, movement to the right caught her eye. Watching Lillith step behind a mausoleum so as not be seen, Rory was confused. She knew of no reason Lillith should be hiding.

✝

The house was full of people as it always was on special occasions. Only this was not one of those gatherings that all enjoyed in this old house.

Sitting on the bed Nikki wondered if she should still go through with the rest of the planned renovations. Another alternative would be to sell the house and buy something smaller. "Maybe I'll sell everything and move into a condo."

A knock on the door startled her, causing Nikki to jump to her feet. It was then that she realized she'd dumped her clothes from her lap onto the floor.

Kirstin didn't wait for an answer. Walking in, she found Nikki standing by the end of the bed dressed in only her skirt and bra.

Nikki knew that by Kirstin's reaction she must've had a scared look on her face.

"Oh honey, I'm sorry, I didn't mean to scare you like that."

"It's all right I guess my mind was just doddling. How long have I been up here?"

Kirstin walked to Nikki slowly. She obviously didn't want to spook her further. "About thirty minutes."

Kirstin had tried not to treat Nikki as a child since Alex's death. Sometimes though, she felt so sorry for her. This was one of those times as she watched Nikki struggling with her top. "Here, let me help you with that sweater."

"Thanks, I can't seem to get things right today." Kirstin couldn't help but notice Nikki looked like a helpless waif.

Kirstin sat down on the bed. Pulling Nikki's sweater down for her, she knew it was time for another of their talks. "Sit down here beside me and let's talk for a few." Kirstin patted the spot on the bed beside her.

"Honey, it's okay to be sad and overwhelmed, but don't give up. You've made it this far so don't give up. Toward the end, I realized all that was going on. Through everything, you survived because you knew you had to. Well, now you can start to live again. You can start again." Kirstin drew a deep breath. Her eyes wanted to shed tears but she wouldn't let them.

"I loved my sister. She had problems none of us could have fixed. What happened did so for a reason. We both now know Alex wasn't whom you were meant to spend your life with. She's still waiting for you. I know it's going to be hard for you because you feel you don't deserve to be happy, but you do. There are several of us who're going to have to live with ourselves for not stepping in and doing anything. That however, is ours to deal with not yours."

Reaching, Nikki took Kirstin's hand. During the past several weeks, Nikki's demeanor changed drastically. She was always open and bubbly. She always spoke her mind, now she was withdrawn. Nikki was no longer whole and Kirstin had no idea how to fix it.

"Please Kirstin, there is nothing to forgive. I did what I had to do. That's why I couldn't ask for your help. I couldn't bear it if anyone was hurt because of me. The flip side of that is why I am so grateful that you've been so supportive."

Nikki walked to the window overlooking the back deck and patio. "Thank you doesn't seem adequate though. The support, care, and love you showed me helped to keep me sane during the past couple of years. But I really did love her, no matter what. She was my world and I don't know what I'm going to do without her. How do I explain that even through it all, she took care of me, very good care? She did love me, in her own way."

Kirstin's heart hurt for Nikki. "I know. You were her princess."

Turning to look at her, Nikki's face showed no emotion. "No, I was her possession."

✝

Nikki knew she had to make the rounds, thanking everyone for coming and for their condolences. However, all she wanted to do was slink away to hide where she couldn't be found.

With the funeral not taking place until two weeks after Alex's death, Nikki's response to the sympathetic hugs had become automatic. Now when she thanked people, she felt nothing. Their sympathy was lost on her.

Approaching her boss, Nikki automatically held out her hand. "Thank you for coming Mark. I really appreciated all that you and Janet have done for me the past several weeks."

Mark drew Nikki into a hug. "Please, if there is anything you need, all you have to do is call us, and we'll be there. You take off as much time as you need. We'll cover everything that needs to be done. I'll even take a look at the paperwork for the two promotions you were working on."

Janet looked at him, then back at Nikki. She tried not to laugh. "Great Mark, that should make her feel real good. Knowing she'll have to clean up your messes when she gets back. Oh don't give me that look dear, everyone knows who really runs the company."

Mark lowered his head in embarrassment. He knew Janet was right. Nikki was the person that everyone turned to for answers. Without her in the office, the first week things had run smoothly, however, the past week was bad. Finally, the day before the funeral Mark told everyone to go, that he was closing the office for the following week to regroup their thoughts. It was a much-needed break for everyone.

When Liz told Nikki of the mess Mark had made of things in the office, she tried not to laugh at him. He tried his best and failed miserably. Luckily, she was there to clean up after him.

Janet put her arm around Nikki's shoulders. "Anytime you need to talk honey or anything, just call me. I'll always be here for you. Please don't worry about anything other than yourself." Mark's stomach took that moment to growl.

Slapping Mark's stomach, Janet pushed him toward the food. "However, I think I better go feed this monster before he gets out of control. We'll check on you later." She hugged Nikki once more, kissing her on the cheek.

Scott wasn't quite sure what to say to Nikki. They had already talked everything through. She told Scott he shouldn't feel blame, but how could he not feel responsible? He had suspected Alex was behind the 'packages and letters' they had received. However, Scott had never wanted to believe it. After all that happened, he willingly went to a therapist twice a week. It was helping him to work through the anger and guilt.

Scott wondered if the hole in his heart would ever heal after all that has been lost. A friend, a confidante, a part of himself was gone, never to return. Scott had to keep reminding himself he wasn't the only one to have lost something in this nightmare. If it wasn't for Tessa and Tabitha, he wouldn't have survived after taking that fatal shot that cost his friend's life.

The woman walking toward Scott had lost a lover, a part of her soul. Would either of them heal?

Life would never be the same even if some day the hurt diminished.

Scott's heart skipped in fear as Nikki approached. "Hi. I… wanted to offer my thoughts and prayers to you once again. If you ever need anything, call Tessa and me. We will always be here for you. You're a part of our family."

Nikki hugged him, knowing it was what they both needed. Each time they spoke Scott tried to hide the blame he felt. When he told her that he blamed himself for not knowing, for being too late to save them, Nikki reprimanded him.

"Thank you Scott, for everything. I mean that sincerely. If it wasn't for you, I wouldn't be alive today. I owe you everything. Thank you doesn't seem quite adequate does it?"

Wrapping her in a hug, Scott couldn't stop the tears. "You know I can't handle it when grown men cry." Nikki held him tightly as they both cried.

"I should have known. She changed so much during the past several years, but I just didn't want to believe that there was trouble. I didn't want to have to do what I did. Nikki, you have to believe me, there was no other way."

Nikki held on to Scott as she would to a lifeline. "It was Alex. She did this to all of us. There was no other way Scott. We know that and none of us blame you one bit for doing what you did. I for one am very thankful that you got there when you did."

A hand touched her shoulder, startling her.

Kirstin stood beside her. "And so am I Scott or we would have lost both of them."

†

Scott watched Nikki walk away. "I know in my head I did what I had to do, but I think it's going to be a long time for my heart to know that. I am just thankful that Lillith got there when she did. Did you find out who hired her to keep an eye on Nikki?"

Kirstin tried to keep the tension out of her voice. "I've had many conversations with Lillith, but she still refuses to tell me who hired her. Only that she'd been told to watch over Nikki to make sure no harm came to her. I do have an idea who it was though. I'm pretty sure it was Rory."

"I'm a little confused. Why would she do that? Besides how did she know?"

She motioned for Scott to follow her into the garage. She wanted to explain as much as she knew. "Liz helped to fill in some of the missing pieces. Rory left and went to L.A., leaving Nikki behind. I personally never bought the reason why she left. I think Rory was in love with her. Knowing Nikki would never leave Alex, she left instead. She must have known what Alex was capable of so she hired Lillith to watch Nikki. Unfortunately, Alex reverted to her old ways. She was just a little cleverer about it so no one saw the bruises until it was too late. Luckily, for us Lillith was there to stall Alex during her rampage. Two things have bothered me though. How did you know something was wrong and how was it all covered up?"

Scott stared at his hands for a moment. They were the hands that had fired the shot that killed his partner, his best friend.

Sighing, he told Kirstin what only two other people knew. "Nikki had her cell phone in her hand. She managed to hit my speed dial number. When I answered and heard Alex shouting, I knew something was very wrong. I got there are fast as I could. I found Lillith on the floor unconscious and bleeding. Alex was holding Nikki against the wall by her throat with a gun to her head. What happened next you already know. As for the other, the captain didn't think it would do any good dragging the family name through the mud. She always was and always will be seen as a good cop, just like her father and his father before him. I'll never understand how she got so bad. I always knew she had a temper, but nothing like…well, like in the end."

Kirstin couldn't imagine what strength it must have taken to pull the trigger. She knew he would have to find peace within himself for what he had done. "As I said, no one blames you. We are very thankful for what you did. You saved Nikki's life and Alex's reputation. For that Scott I will be forever thankful. I hope you know that you are a dear friend and a member of this family."

Looking out the window of the garage, Kirstin tried to calm her nerves. "Her entire life she was spoiled rotten, always getting her own way. Alex had a volatile temper for as long as I could remember. She tried to control it, but sometimes she failed miserably. I've never seen her so possessive though, not like she was with Nikki. I think something snapped in her when she was shot. We may never know. She was my sister. I loved her no matter what. I would've done anything for her. I however, will never condone what she did. Alex knew she was in trouble. She should have gotten help."

It would be a long road of healing. Each of them knew they would have to help support one another in any way they could. With both of them crying, Kirstin pulled him in for a hug. "Thank you Scott, thank you."

✝

In the back of Nikki's mind, she heard the doorbell ringing. It announced yet another person arriving to pay his or her respects. She was so tired. "You're right Kirstin. My head is ready to explode. I have a migraine starting, I think I'll go lay down for a few minutes."

Turning, Nikki stopped dead. She had not seen her in what seemed like decades. Everything around Nikki seemed to fade away. All she could see was Rory.

Nikki's mind raged with anger. Rory was even more beautiful than before. Her eyes were mesmerizing. Rory looked like she still worked out every day.

Nikki had forgotten she was so tall. Her hair as always styled so perfectly and black as night. Why now? Why come now?

Their eyes met. As she felt tears running down her face, they likewise streamed down Rory's. Taking a step toward her, Nikki needed to know if Rory was truly there or if her brain had taken a vacation. Nikki felt her hands start to tremble.

Looking down at her hands, they looked foreign to Nikki. She thought for sure someone else was controlling them as one of them raised toward Rory. Nikki's body leaned into Rory's of its own accord.

To those watching it looked as if Nikki were raising her hand to caress the other woman's face when all of a sudden she slapped Rory as hard as she could. Nikki didn't know what happened to her. She swore she would never lay a hand on another human being ever again, but Nikki couldn't have stopped her hand if she had tried.

Rory's head snapped to the right then back again. She continued looking straight into Nikki's eyes, daring her to do it again. Or was she begging Nikki to? Was this Rory's penance, to be humiliated in front of everyone? Rory did nothing to defend herself as Nikki brought her hand back around for a second strike.

This time though Nikki's hand stopped midair. Looking from her hand to the beautiful woman standing in front of her the anger in Nikki deflated. The hand dropped back to her side. Raising it once more, she could almost feel those around her cringing, expecting another whack at any second.

Nikki was positive what they witnessed instead was a relief. She laid her hand upon the taller woman's face, stepping so close their bodies touched.

Nikki looked up into eyes that were the darkest violet she had ever seen. They were so dark they were almost black. The feeling of silky soft skin under her fingers was exquisite. Rory leaned into the caress. Nikki couldn't think straight. She then asked what she had wanted to so long ago.

"Why?"

Rory opened her eyes. Nikki saw nothing more than love and desire. "Because... I fell in love with you."

Rory caught Nikki in her arms as she lost consciousness.

✝

Nikki's mind felt cloudy. With trouble concentrating, her thoughts slowly returned to the hell they had escaped. Before opening her eyes, her brain registered another presence in the room. Nikki hoped it was Liz or Kirstin. Sighing, she turned her head away from the person sitting next to her on the bed.

Nikki told herself if they realized she was waking up, they would say something to her. That way she would know who it was before opening her eyes. If it was anyone other than Liz or Kirstin, Nikki would pretend to fall back asleep.

Not only did the person not say anything, but Nikki swore she heard light snoring coming from the person. Nikki spoke quietly, "Oh well, might as well grin and bear it as they say. So I passed out, what's so embarrassing about that?"

Nikki slowly opened her eyes, realizing she must've been out for some time. The late afternoon sun was casting shadows across the room. The house was eerily quiet.

Nikki turned her head looking at the sleeping person next to her. As she did so, Nikki raised herself into her elbows to get a better look at who it was.

"Shit!" The statement hung in the air long enough to make Nikki regret making any noise as she realized who it was.

Cringing, Nikki watched as Rory slowly open her eyes. She had awakened her. Rory sat upright with her back against the headboard. Gazing at one another, each of them was afraid to be the first to break the spell.

Slowly Nikki's hand cradled Rory's face. "Where have you been all my life?"

Rory laid her hand over Nikki's. "Alone"

Frowning she looked into Rory's eyes. "Funny, I've been in hell the past few years."

Nikki dropped her hand. "A Hell…that you could've saved me from. Instead, you walked away. It's too late now. I have nothing to offer you. You're too late. Go back to whoever you were with last, love her not me."

Rory heard hollowness in Nikki's voice that was never there before. There were to be no tears. By this point in life, Nikki had shed all that she could. Standing up, Nikki walked across the room.

Rory stood behind her, close enough that she knew Nikki could feel her breath on her ear. It however was not nearly enough to breach the wall between them. Laying her hand on Nikki's shoulder, she felt her cringe. "Nikki…."

"No! How am I supposed to even care about you? You left when I needed you most. Worst of all though is that you lied to me. I needed your friendship and support, and you lied!"

Even though Rory expected what Nikki had said, hurt nonetheless.

"Get out."

A deathly quiet fell in the room, then in the house as Rory closed the front door behind her, leaving Nikki alone.

As Rory left the house, her heart was breaking. She thought she had made the right decision to come and open her heart to Nikki. Now she was not so sure. Rory knew she had made a terrible mistake leaving so long ago. Thinking that Nikki would be better off without her, Rory thought Nikki could handle Alex on her own. "I gambled that Alex would change and lost."

Lillith waited outside until all the others left the house.

Several hours earlier Lillith watched as Rory entered the house to pay her respects. Before going in Rory had knocked on Lillith's truck window. Lillith told Rory that she would wait until later.

After everyone left except Rory and Kirstin, slowly Lillith climbed the steps.

A smiling Kirstin met Lillith at the door. "I am glad you're here. I need to go home and check on the kids. Nikki didn't take seeing Rory too well. She passed out. She's upstairs sleeping. Rory decided to pull up a chair beside her. I really don't know how she'll handle waking up and seeing her again. Could you stay to make sure she is okay, at least until I get back? Help yourself to the food in the fridge, there's plenty." With that said, Kirstin made a rapid exit.

Lillith had just finishing eating a sandwich when she heard the raised voices. They were followed by loud booted footsteps rushing down the stairs. Then the front door opened and closed. There was only one person it could've been since everyone else had already left. Lillith peered out the window in the front door to see Rory standing beside the truck. She then silently made her way upstairs to check on Nikki.

Pausing outside the bedroom door Lillith suddenly felt unsure. Unsure of what her future held. Lillith had strong feelings for Nikki. She asked herself though, did she have any right bringing Nikki into her life when all she ever knew was the darker side of life? For to know Lillith would be even worse. Her life was lived in the darkest, farthest reaches of Hell.

As Lillith raised her hand to knock she peered into the room through the half-open door. Nikki stood by the bed with a lockbox in front of her. She watched as Nikki unlocked and opened the box.

When Nikki pulled a gun from it, Lillith reacted without thought. She rushed into the room. "No!"

The sudden presence of another person and the shout startled Nikki. Out of reflex, she pulled on the trigger and the gun went off. Nikki screamed, throwing the gun to the floor.

"Oh, God…the safety…I didn't know it was loaded."

Lillith put her arms around Nikki, pulling her away from the bed where the bullet had impacted. She held Nikki tightly, trying to soothe her, whispering that everything was okay now.

Lillith didn't want to think about why Nikki was pulling a gun from the box. The only thing that mattered was that she was unharmed. "It is okay, darling. It was just an accident, nothing more. We will get through this together, okay?"

"I'm fine, really. I just…I just…" Nikki tried to pull away from her but Lillith held tight. "Oh, God….what was I thinking? I just couldn't stand the pain and loneliness anymore."

"Nikki, you will never be alone as long as I live." She pulled Nikki's face up, lowering her head to kiss her.

Nikki pushed slightly away from her. "I don't know if I can, I don't know if I have it in me any longer. Yet I do care for you."

✝

In her heart Rory knew she could've tried to take Nikki away from Alex. What would the cost have been though? Nikki had been terrified that Alex would hurt anyone who stepped in her way. The day Rory confronted her, Alex had sworn on her life that she would change, never harming Nikki again in any way.

With everything spinning out of control, Rory paused, leaning against the truck.

"What have I done? Why did I believe that bitch? The condition Nikki was in was as much her fault as it was Alex's." Rory could do nothing other than lay her head on the truck and sob. "Oh God, I could've saved her and I didn't."

The snow fell covering Rory in tiny white flakes. She stood having a full-blown self-loathing party. Rory hated herself as much as she hated Alex.

Feeling the tears freezing on her face, Rory knew she couldn't just leave. Even though it was broken, her heart truly belonged to Nikki– she just had to prove it somehow. Pushing away from the truck, she knew what she had to do. Wondering when it had started to snow, Rory brushed the snow from her sleeves.

Rory had taken one step from the truck when she heard it. It sounded like a gunshot. Taking only a second for the sound to register, her reflex was automatic. Rory sprinted toward the house, up the steps and through the door.

✝

They heard a throat clearing and turned toward the door. Rory knew the embarrassment at walking in on a private moment showed as her face flushed red. "I, um, well I see everything is okay here. I'll be going. I guess congrats are in order." She started for the stairs.

Lillith rushed into the hallway to stop Rory from leaving. "Wait, Ror…I never meant to have feelings for her." Lillith felt the guilt seep into her.

Rory turned and looked at her life-long friend. "No, it truly is okay. The only thing I want in life is her happiness. If that's with you, then that's the way it has to be. Just promise me this, that you will protect her heart and soul. She has a lot to give and has never been given the chance. Love her with all you are. Remember though, that first you must tell her who and what you are because there must never be any secrets or lies between you. If you don't think you can do that, you need to walk away now and never look back."

Lillith looked down at her hands, which from years of training had become steel fists. "I would do anything for her, I would die for her, and I will never abandon her. Even if she cannot accept what my life has been up to this point, I will never leave her. I will not do it, I cannot do it."

Rory started down the steps. "Even knowing she may never be capable of loving you?"

She answered immediately from her heart, not needing to think about it. "Yes."

Rory reached the bottom of the stairs. "Good, she will need you to be her rock. Good luck to both of you."

Rory left that day never looking back. She knew there was nothing she could've done to change the outcome. Rory had made her destiny. Her future was to be spent alone. She spoke to the two of them off and on, but never saw Nikki again, calling on Lillith only when necessary.

✝

Through months of therapy, Nikki let go of the fears that had ruled her life for so many years. She was able to release the anger that had controlled her. If she hadn't let go, it would've destroyed her. She didn't want to end up alone and bitter as her sister had.

Throughout her sessions, she ran the gamut of emotions. During that time, one thing remained constant, her growing feelings for Lillith. No matter what, she stood by Nikki, never judging her and as a result she had almost died.

Nikki had to forgive herself before she could do the same for Alex. A part of her would always love her and belong to her. Nikki knew in the end that loving Alex wouldn't be enough, just as she knew she couldn't have stopped her. Nikki admitted that what had happened could never have been changed.

Letting go of the betrayal she felt toward Rory, Nikki accepted that it was she herself who had pushed her away and not Rory who had left her alone in her darkest moments. Even with Nikki telling her repeatedly, Rory still blamed herself for what happened. Rory had stepped aside as she watched the woman whom she loved fall in love with someone else. Rory did nothing to stop it. It was the right thing to do. Nikki knew Rory would never forget that day of reckoning as long as she lived.

Many times Nikki looked back to that day – the turning point in her life, as well as Lillith's and Rory's.

†

Lillith kept true to her word. She was with Nikki during the good days and through the rough nights when Nikki would wake screaming from a nightmare. She moved into the house with Nikki, but not into the same bedroom. Lillith took her to and from her sessions with the therapist, even attending several of them with her.

Lillith had also pledged to tell her life to the woman who held her heart. She confessed her sins, not just during the nights they sat awake unable to sleep, but during those sessions that helped both of them come to terms with themselves.

Lillith related to Nikki how she had come to have no family. There had been a family get together during the summer break from the professional bull riding season so that her sister Dakota and brother Jack could be there as well. Lillith had watched as Dakota's wife RJ and their child, the last to arrive, entered through the back door of the house along with the town sheriff, just moments before the gunfire was heard and fire claimed the house and the lives of all within it. Young Lillith had been upset with her mother and was in the hayloft of the barn pouting, which spared her life. Or did it? The city had wanted their land and her family had refused to sell and then suddenly they were all gone. Lillith became angry at life and humanity. That was when Lars, an aging hitman who had been looking for a protégé, had found her and molded her into what she became.

Even knowing who Lillith was, Nikki never faltered. Running from her would have been the coward's way out. Instead, she chose to fight for a future with her. Nikki now knew what less than a handful of people knew about Lillith. That she had spent the better part of her life bringing about death, as a killer for hire.

✝

A little more than two years after Alex's death, Lillith sat in their favorite Italian restaurant with the woman she had come to love beside her. Surrounding them were family and friends.

Lillith stood addressing the table, gathering everyone's attention.

"I am a woman of few words, so I will make this quick. These past two years have brought many changes to all our lives. We have all grown older, wiser and found that we are an unbreakable family. Scott, Tessa, Liz, Mark, Janet, Tom and Kirstin…I want to thank all of you for accepting me into this family. I have not had a family in my life since I was a child. I want to thank all of you for coming here today."

She turned to Nikki. "Nikki, I, well… you know how I feel about you. I have only one last wish in life to fulfill."

She pulled a small box from her pocket. Lillith felt as if time had stopped as she looked into Nikki's eyes. No one else existed outside the two of them. After what felt like a lifetime came the words. "Nikki, will you marry me? Will you be one with me for all time?"

Lillith heard through Nikki's sobs the one answer that would finally deliver her soul from the blackness and desolation that she had existed in for so long.

"Yes, oh yes."

"Mark. Nikki and I are going to need a month off after the wedding. I plan on showing her Ireland in style."

Not since Lillith was a small girl, playing cops and robbers with her father, had her eyes twinkled. The blue eyes, that held nothing but love for Nikki, now out-shined every star in the sky.

Everyone at the table watched as Lillith's eyes shifted and her mouth dropped open. Tears streamed down her face. Their eyes followed the path of Lillith's and took in the sight of a ruggedly handsome woman, with a scarred face, walking toward their table. She looked like a very young Lillith, even with the same blue eyes.

With all eyes on her the young lady walked up to Lillith and stopped. "Hi, Aunt Lillith, I'm your niece, RJ."

Lillith sat down with an audible thud. "By the Gods…it was you that day, photographing the tanker."

The younger woman leaned to kiss her aunt on the cheek. "Yes, and I have already forgiven you. You must now forgive yourself for that day."

Epilogue

She wanted so much to be enjoying her sixth anniversary with Nikki. Instead, Lillith found herself packing while calling in a favor to get her to North Carolina. All the while, she nodded to a very pregnant and hormonally pissed off wife. This emergency call could not have come at a worse time. This pregnancy was not going as easily as the first had.

"Thank you very much. I should be there in thirty."

Lillith turned to Nikki. "I am so sorry, my love. I need to find this guy. I was called because I can find him in a matter of hours."

"Which you did, now let them go get him and take him back to New York. They don't need you to do that. Besides, he sounds dangerous. I can't believe he tried to kill her. That's horrible. His own family…. How disgusting…." Nikki shook her head.

Lillith sat on the edge of the bed, caressing Nikki's swollen belly. "Babe, I promised Jack I would take care of it. I will only be gone for a couple of days at the most. RJ is on her way here so you will not be alone. I am sorry, my love."

Nikki sighed. "I know I'm being silly. I just feel like a beached whale. God, who would have thought… twins. From what I can gather, they run in my family. Just make me one promise….”

Lillith kissed her. “Anything, my little beach ball.”

“I’m ignoring that comment, for now. Darling, please don’t hurt him. That’s not you anymore.”

Lillith smiled, which made Nikki beam.

“I love your smile darling, come home soon.”

“I will, I promise. I will deliver Ronald the weasel to the New York State Police and be home before you know it.”

Not all things in life go according to plan.

About the Author

Alane Hotchkin

Alane Hothkin; If anyone knows where the birthplace of oil is in North America you will know exactly where I am talking about. I was born in Oil City, PA and later lived in Pittsburgh. You say do not know where Oil City is. Well imagine a tiny town population "two" directly between Pittsburgh & Erie, PA. I grew up with family always around (mostly male) and all with wicked senses of humor. My one cousin one day decided to see if his father's (my uncle) car would float in the retention pond.

Okay, so now you also know where I got my sense of humor. My earliest childhood memory is driving to the store with my favorite uncle to buy his cigarettes & booze in his HUGE Cadillac with the top down, while listening to an eight track of Dolly Parton's Coat of Many Colors and so a little girl's education was started. <LOL>

Side Note: Finally, in 2005, I had to admit to myself and unwillingly to others that well….I'm a country hick even though all my life I tried to be a city girl. <LOL>

Other Books from Affinity

Through the Darkness—Erin O'Reilly Becca Cameron is a loner—by choice. She lives in a hundred year old farmhouse built by her great grandfather. A tragic accident in her home a year earlier drove away her lover, and Becca tries to accept what she cannot change and hang on to the belief that love can conquer all.

Chase Hunter, had a meteoric rise in the Eastman Corporation and was, at thirty-four, the youngest vice-president. To Chase, her work was all consuming leaving little time for friends or lovers. There was simply no place in her life for anything but her job.

When Becca and Chase meet at their work place, the attraction is spontaneous. Life begins to look brighter for both women as work takes a second seat to romance.

Unknown to either woman, someone is watching their every move…

Will passion outweigh doubt? Can love conqueror fear?

Beginning of the End—Alane Hotchkin What happens when life doesn't go exactly as you planned and you must protect others from your own fate? Escaping a horrific childhood, Nikki longed to find happily ever after in adulthood. What she found was Hell. Or did it find her? Finding the courage to break the cycle of betrayal, she opens her heart one last time. Alex lived a childhood others dreamed of. Her father never once denied the young rebel a thing. All her life she dreamed of protecting others; to follow in her father's footsteps. Soon though she learned sex and fists made the most powerful of weapons. Alex controls the women in her life through fear and sex, will breaking the cycle be too much to overcome? Will loving Nikki be enough to change her, or is Alex beyond help?

Alex would give Nikki the world, but at what price? When a person's tightly controlled reality snaps what then…? This is the Beginning of the End for one of them and the ultimate sacrifice for the other. But who is who in this game of life?

Galveston 1900: Swept Away—Linda Crist On September 7-8, 1900, the island of Galveston, Texas, was destroyed by a hurricane, or 'tropical cyclone', as it was called in those days. This story is a fictional account of Mattie and Rachel, two women who lived there, and their lives during the time of the 'great storm'. Forced to flee from her family at a young age, Rachel Travis finds a home and livelihood on the island of Galveston. Independent, friendly, and yet often lonely, only one other person knows the dark secret that haunts her. Madeline "Mattie" Crockett is trapped in a loveless marriage, convinced that her fate is sealed. She never dares to dream of true happiness, until Rachel Travis comes walking into her life.   As emotions come to light, the storm of Mattie's marriage converges with the very real hurricane. Can they survive, and build the life they both dream of?

This second edition of one of Linda Crist's best-loved novels maintains the original story, while incorporating some reader-pleasing passages that were cut from the first edition. As an added bonus, the short story "Something to Celebrate" is included at the end of the novel, detailing further adventures of Rachel and Mattie.

Rapture: Sins of the Sinners—A. C. Henley & Fran Heckrotte A serial killer is targeting young lesbians throughout the state of Texas.Texas Ranger Cochetta Lovejoy is assigned to the case. Convinced she knows who is committing the murders, Ranger Lovejoy is willing to do whatever it takes to put the perpetrator behind bars--even if it means stretching the limits of the law by manipulating the judicial system. Detective Agnes Kelly-Elliott is one of Ft. Worth Police Department's finest investigators. When Ranger Lovejoy appears on the crime scene of a recent murder, Agnes fears a dark secret that, if revealed, could destroy her family ties, and end her career. This is a dark, gritty, graphic tale of desire gone awry, and flawed characters looking for redemption in all the wrong places.

Till There Was You—S. Anne Gardner Julia is a woman used to power and is not afraid to use it or impose her will to get her way. She appears to have the world but a part of her is empty and cold as a frozen tundra. Julia rides in the mornings to clear her head and to make plans for what she is about to set in motion. Theodora, known as Teddy, is trying to put together a marriage filled with uncertainties. She felt once upon a time that she would have a great love but that has eluded her. One morning these two women meet and from the first instance, it is explosive. The attraction is undeniable, the fears very real and the end without question will change them both forever.

Denial—Jackie Kennedy Time spent in Somalia has Doctor Celeste Cameron accustomed to living and working in a war zone. Coming back home to America, Celeste is glad to see the end of the peril she has been in—or so she thinks. Danger seems to follow Celeste and she finds it in the shape of Amy. What Celeste feels for Amy scares her more than anything she has faced in war zones. Amy has the same feelings, but is in denial and vows to marry Josh, Celeste's twin brother, no matter what. When fate brings them together again, will they give in to their mutual attraction or will they once again deny what they feel.

Absolution—S. Anne Gardner Games of the rich and famous, love, lust, and forbidden passions weave this tale that play out through decades and the world. The close ties the Alcalas have to the royal house of Spain provide them with an unspoken untouchable policy. Their passions and their secrets are about to come to light with a force that cannot be stopped. In this whirlwind is Cristina Uraca Alacala who is searching for a truth that has been denied to her most of her life and she must find. She is not unlike her family; Cristina does not stop until she gets what she wants. In the fog lies the truth that she must travel through to find.

In this tale wealthy socialite Annais Francesca D'Autremond is a pivotal person of interest in Cristina's search for the truth. When these two women meet they find themselves drawn together by something greater than themselves. As the truth of a hidden past becomes clearer their passions grow beyond the realm of the no return instead of a status quo. Both tied together by destiny; will both survive the onslaught of past and present passions?

In Name Only—JM Dragon—Sequel to The Fix-it Girl Can an agreement forged out of necessity actually work?

An Affair of Love—S. Anne Gardner From a dark past, a forbidden love, a secret comes. Among the confusion and the chaos of an unwanted reality, two women find something they neither want nor can deny.

Desert Heat—Dannie Marsden For Luce Diamond, an undercover policewoman, her life is in shambles. Her longtime lover left her and an automobile accident that resulted in a child's death haunts her.

Taming the Wolff—Del Robertson ONLY ONE WOMAN...HAS THE POWER...TO TAME THE WOLFF...

Private Dancer—TJ Vertigo Reece Corbett grew up on the mean streets on New York City, abused, used and in trouble with the law. Faith Ashford grew up wealthy, with all the creature comforts that money provides. When they meet fireworks begin.

Miriam and Esther—Sherry Barker Miriam thought her life would play out in the bustling metropolis of Dallas, but after a life-changing accident, she moves to the small town of Cool Lake, Texas to get her head on straight and regain her senses.

McKee—A.C. Henley Private Investigator Quinlan McKee has returned to Los Angeles after a three-year absence, only to find herself embroiled in a world of child slavery and police corruption.

Bailey's Run—Ali Spooner Bailey Chambers mourns the loss of her lover, Nessa, in an unsolved carjacking. When Tommy, Bailey's brother becomes a victim of a gay bashing, Bailey assumes his case will be handled the same way as her lover's—lackadaisically.

Desi Dexter assigned to Tommy's case, feels Bailey's disdain toward her and her partner. Through tenacious police work, Desi, is able to uncover the reason for Bailey's attitude, and convinces her that she is sincere in solving the case.

Mutual attraction sparks, and before they can move forward with their fledging romance, Desi, and her partner Braxton, uncover the presence of a serial killer.

What will happen to Bailey, when, Desi, becomes engrossed in another case, can their relationship survive?

E-Books, Print, Free e-books

Visit our website for more publications available online.

www.affinityebooks.com

Published by Affinity E-Book Press NZ LTD

Canterbury, New Zealand
Registered Company 2517228